8/19

Bloomfield 3/19
Low 5/19
Houghton 6/19

☞ P9-CFL-477

MOONBEAMS IN A JAR

When Chloe Potter wishes on a star that she'll find a man who'll accept her and her noisy dachshund, Wilma, almost immediately she meets Ryan Green and his boisterous basset hound, Fred. But Ryan's job as a photographer means that when he's not in the middle of a war zone, he's trying to catch just the right light at the top of Mount Snowdon. Chloe wants stability and knows she has to move on. But then a once-in-a-lifetime trip unexpectedly brings them together once again . . .

Books by Christine Stovell
in the Linford Romance Library:

ONLY TRUE IN FAIRY TALES

CHRISTINE STOVELL

◆

MOONBEAMS IN A JAR

Complete and Unabridged

LINFORD
Leicester

First published in Great Britain in 2018
Choc Lit Limited
Surrey

First Linford Edition
published 2019
Choc Lit Limited
Surrey

A catalogue record for this book is available from the British Library.

ISBN 978–1–4448–3971–5

Published by
F. A. Thorpe (Publishing)
Anstey, Leicestershire

Set by Words & Graphics Ltd.
Anstey, Leicestershire
Printed and bound in Great Britain by
T. J. International Ltd., Padstow, Cornwall

This book is printed on acid-free paper

Dedication

For Harry, Phoebe, Evelyn and Kimmy who fill my jar with moonbeams.

Acknowledgements

One summer evening when Tom, my husband, asked me where in the world I'd like to go if I could hop on a plane the next day, I never expected him to surprise me with the trip to Hong Kong I'd dreamed of. I'm afraid my initial reaction was one of shock, but Tom, you were right and I was wrong because sometimes we have to be bold to make dreams come true. Thank you, my darling, for a magical holiday and the memories that wove their way into this novella.

As always, I'm profoundly grateful to everyone at Choc Lit — my fellow authors and the hardworking team — for their continued support. Thank you also to the readers on the Tasting Panel who passed this book for publication: Lizzy D, Cordy S, Susan D, Jenny M, Sam E, Margaret M, Rachel D, Barbara B, Isabella T,

Katie P, Jo O and Elisabeth H. Three cheers to all of you! Finally, a huge thank you to my loving family — I couldn't do any of this without you.

1

As the heat of a long summer day rose up to meet the purple clouds, Chloe Potter sat perched at the end of a creaky wooden pontoon, swinging her legs. She watched the light fade determined to soak up every last minute of what had been an unforgettable holiday. Only two weeks ago, she'd sat in the very same spot and wondered if the ache in her chest was her broken heart or her ribs straining with the effort of holding back tears. And now? Yes, she *was* apprehensive about everything in store for her when she went back to everyday life and, if she was honest, she *did* feel a pang of regret that the magic had to end. Quite a big pang, actually. But as for hoping the dream could go on? Well, that was like wishing she could swing on a star. Some things were forever out of reach.

She glanced at Wilma, sitting beside her, who rolled her eyes making it perfectly clear that she was done with sitting shivering in the twilight.

'All right, I know you want something to eat,' said Chloe, getting to her feet. 'And I'm sorry you're fed up — but, be fair, waiting for me isn't that much of a hardship given everything I've done for you. So, come on then, let's go.'

Wilma took a couple of delicate steps then froze at the sight of a particularly wide gap between the wooden planks of the pontoon.

Chloe tutted at her. 'Come on, you should be over this by now. There's no way you'll fall through.'

Wilma looked uncertain.

'You know, Guy said you'd always be a liability,' said Chloe, who had resigned herself to packing and wanted to get it done. 'Maybe I should have listened when he said it was time to ditch you, eh?'

And then where would she have been? Snuggled up in Guy's fabulous flat with its pale carpets, cream sofas, opulent French bed and smooth white sheets, that's where. Not licking her wounds in a in a last-minute bargain holiday cottage in the less than glamorous resort of Little Spitmarsh.

To begin with, Guy seemed to think Chloe was joking when she'd told him she couldn't possibly abandon Wilma. Then he'd turned quite nasty and accused her of never loving him in the first place if she was really choosing Wilma with her bad breath, horrible manners and evil farts over him.

Wilma shook her red head and looked up at her with such deep devotion that Chloe forgot to be stern and bent to scoop the little dachshund into her arms.

'Who needs cream sofas anyway?' she muttered, stroking Wilma's soft coat. Beyond the end of the pontoon, Venus was rising, shining her light on the still waters of the creek. 'But next time,' Chloe wished out loud, 'please could you send me a guy who loves dogs instead of Guy who hates them?'

Wilma, apparently determined to seal the deal with a heartfelt lick, attempted to scramble up her T-shirt to reach her cheek. One of the dog's back feet, struggling for purchase, clipped the pocket of Chloe's jeans and sent her phone skidding perilously close to the edge of the decking.

'Sheesh, you like to live dangerously, don't you, dog?' she muttered. 'I might've had to think twice about Guy's advice if that had gone in the water.' Tucking Wilma securely under one arm, she knelt, leant forwards and was cautiously stretching out her hand when something thundered up behind her and poked her in the bottom.

'No, Fred, no! How many times do I have to tell you? That's not the way to greet a lady!'

From her position, sprawled out on the pontoon, Chloe noticed that Wilma had gone for complete capitulation; she'd rolled onto her back and was shamelessly showing her tummy to a large

4

basset hound. When she turned her head the other way Chloe could see a pair of rugged boots and then a deep masculine voice asked if she was all right.

'Just about,' Chloe said, grabbing her phone with relief. 'My whole life's on this at the moment, I don't know what I'd do without it.'

'Perhaps it's a sign that you should change your life.'

Chloe felt a flicker of elation, but was careful not to fuel it with foolish dreams and false hopes. Two weeks ago when her self-esteem had been at rock bottom, she would have scoffed at the notion of a holiday romance. In fact, she'd deliberately chosen the bolthole in the back of beyond for its seclusion and its location barely a ten-minute walk from Campion's Creek, a meandering waterway through the Little Spitmarsh backwaters.

Her one reservation was that the squat black-stained clapboard bungalow sat in the grounds of an unpretentious Victorian house making her vulnerable to intrusive questions from any inquisitive owner. So it was a relief when the key-holder, a vivacious flame-haired young woman appropriately called Tansy, reassured her that she was most unlikely to be disturbed as the holiday cottage belonged to her cousin, a landscape photographer, who was out in the wilds on an assignment.

Except that on the very first evening a jeep turned up in the drive of the house, a hall light spilled out through the open door and a tall, well-built man with untamed dark hair and a dense beard came running out in pursuit of a determined basset hound hell-bent on making inappropriate advances to Wilma. The apologetic grin he bestowed on her, once they'd separated the dogs, suggested — from what she could see of him in the dwindling light and beneath all the hair — that he was really rather attractive. Ryan Green was home.

'Look, I know you're on a holiday and you probably want to get away from it all, but if you fancy it, you and

Wilma could join me and Fred for dinner?' he'd suggested. 'It would make up for Fred's behaviour and there's plenty of food to go round.'

'That does sound nice.' Chloe had nodded. She hadn't really felt like cooking, especially when there was a very attractive man offering to do it for her.

Wilma hadn't been in any hurry to leave Fred though so Ryan had offered to look after her while Chloe sorted out a couple of things in the cottage. Before Chloe could warn him, he bent and lifted Wilma into his arms. 'Pretty lady,' he'd commented, smiling.

To Chloe's horror Wilma had simply returned the compliment in her usual way; she'd batted her lashes and farted at him. So when, Ryan just laughed, Chloe decided that any man who could put up with Wilma was ahead of the game.

'Wow! Pretty lady who packs a punch,' she heard him say, admiringly, as she hurried off to drag a brush through her hair and put on some lipstick. 'She's adorable, isn't she, quite a girl.'

Now, still sprawled out on the decking, clutching her phone, Chloe marvelled at how that evening had not only marked the start of an exhilarating break from real life, but also from her own normally rather cautious and sensible character. *That* Chloe knew awful things happened, that life could be cruel and so did everything she could to keep hurt at bay. Of course, when she went back to her ordinary life, she would be even more careful before getting involved in a new relationship — she'd had no idea that her ex, Guy, would turn out to be quite so prissy about Wilma — but in Ryan, she'd met a dog-loving guy who'd given her a glimpse of the fun-loving Chloe she could be in different circumstances.

But all holidays had to end.

She rolled over, took the hand Ryan offered and let him help her to her feet.

'So, what's next?' he asked softly.

Chloe felt a sudden thump in her chest and was glad it was too dark for him to read her expression. She took a deep breath and forced herself to sound upbeat. 'Pack, early night . . . and then back to harsh reality. I'll chase up some work contacts, look for somewhere to rent, pick myself up and carry on.'

'But not exactly from where you left off?'

'No. No, I've learned my lesson. It's me and Wilma first now. I'll find a new job, somewhere to live and we'll live happily ever after. Perhaps you'll think of us walking round the local park when you and Fred are battling the elements out in the wilderness?' Her attempt at a laugh caught in her throat as she imagined him in a future that was nothing to do with her, a future, she reminded herself, that really wasn't any of her concern given that the beauty of their two-week relationship meant it would never be put to the test of ordinary life.

'Chloe . . . '

She saw a shadowy movement as he pushed back his hair.

'I travel a great deal. It's one of the aspects of my job that I love; spending lots of time in the remotest parts of the UK in all seasons and all weathers.'

She nodded, even though he probably couldn't see. His landscape photography portfolio was remarkable, no wonder he was able to make a living from it. 'I know,' she agreed.

'But *you're* going to push some boundaries too from now on, aren't you? You *will* take that trip to Hong Kong, won't you? Before you get stuck in a . . . '

'Rut?' Compared to his, her life must seem very dull.

'Routine.'

'You watched me make the booking, Ryan. My last big splurge before I settle down and save for a deposit. With a bit of luck, I might be able to buy a flat in, ooh, about fifty years time and then I'll sit in my armchair and think about the intrepid outdoor photographer who made me feel good about myself and set me on my feet again.'

For a moment he just stood there, as if he was weighing up what to say, but Chloe didn't want him to feel forced into making promises he couldn't keep. She stepped forwards and they kissed until Wilma and Fred started getting impatient and gave a great chorus of howls that echoed across the water.

'I came to tell you dinner's ready, that is, if you're happy to eat with me tonight,' he said, breaking off and stroking her cheek.

'I'm happy,' she said, taking his hand as they followed the dogs along the pontoon where Wilma, she noticed, wasn't making a single protest about the gaps. Venus twinkled above them, a lucky star, so Chloe decided to be daring.

'Ryan?'

He squeezed her hand.

'Do you remember what I told you about my dad getting married again?'

'To the wicked step-mother-in-waiting?'

Chloe sighed. 'I'm sure she isn't

wicked, I just can't imagine anyone else in Mum's place, that's the problem.'

'Which is why you're so keen to move out of your dad's house and find alternative accommodation?'

'Mmm.' In normal circumstances, she would have left home much sooner, but after her mum had died, her dad had cut such a lonely figure it suited them both for her to continue living there. 'I think it would be better for everyone if Dad and Emma started their married life without me hanging around like the ghost at the wedding feast. On which subject . . . Would you like to be my 'plus one' on the big day? I know it's a huge ask, but you'd be doing me a massive favour. Saving me from those pitying glances for a start and it would certainly make the day go quicker. It's not until the middle of November so you don't have to answer now, but — '

'Chloe.'

'Yes?'

He spoke gently. 'My diary's already

looking full in November. I've been commissioned to take a series of photos of British mountains in winter. That'll mean a lot of hanging around waiting for the right weather conditions. My work means that my life's pretty nomadic, I don't want to commit to a date only to let you down at the last minute.'

'Oh.' She felt the heat rush to her face then ebb away just as quickly, leaving her cold and disappointed. 'Of course, I understand. It's fine. I just thought I'd ask.'

'Come on, let's get inside,' he murmured, leading her along the narrow path through the grassy dunes towards his house. The day's warmth had faded now and Chloe shivered as she waited for him to open the front door. A delicious smell of something simmering in the oven greeted them as Ryan led her through to the kitchen and opened a bottle of wine.

He raised his glass to her, but his expression was troubled. 'You asked me to think of you when you're not here and, right now, I don't know how I'm going to stop thinking about you, Chloe Potter . . . I know you've had setbacks, but things are changing for you. I understand why you're apprehensive about your dad's wedding, but it might turn out to be a lot easier than you imagine. Me being there, even if I was free on the day, might put undue pressure on us both, don't you think?'

Chloe took a large gulp of her wine to hide her disappointment.

'You've got a lot of exciting opportunities coming up and you don't know where they'll take you,' he added reasonably. 'Life can turn in an instant, believe me, so why not give yourself some space?'

Chloe's vision blurred and the wine turned to vinegar in her mouth as she forced herself to smile. Oh, she knew all about life-changing events, but now wasn't the time to tell him. Even so, he was right about one thing; it was wishful thinking to believe that their holiday romance could have led to anything permanent. Besides, the clues had been there all the time. Frankly, a glance at his website might have given her a hint; *Ryan Green is a professional photographer based in East Anglia's Little Spitmarsh. Ryan specialises in landscape, adventure, sporting and cultural events and has undertaken a wide variety of commissions.*

But not weddings.

2

Three Months Later . . .

Chloe opened her eyes to find that while she'd been sleeping, the darkness had given way to a milky opalescent light. Forty thousand feet below her, mile upon mile of snow-covered peaks rose up like islands through a sea of clouds. Siberia, she realised, craning her neck to see more of the unbelievable view. She had so much to look forward to; a brand new start in London *and* an exciting career opportunity. But first, after only dreaming of it, she really was on her way to the Far East.

All right, part of her was sorry that Ryan, the man who'd encouraged her to follow her dream, wasn't there beside her, sharing in her excitement, but that only made her even more determined to make the most of every second of her holiday. Everything was going to be perfect, she told herself, blinking away the sudden tears and swallowing hard on the lump in her throat. All she needed to do was stick to her plan and put Ryan right out of her head. Thinking about him only left her feeling as deserted as the icy wasteland beneath the plane and almost as cold as the mountain tops. Ryan had been generous, impulsive and in two all too brief weeks, had turned her life from mundane to magical. But falling for him had been like chasing a rainbow or catching the wind. How could you hold onto someone who was never there?

Oh, but how the memory of him clung to her. She could even smell the sandalwood and cedar scent of his soap. If she hadn't known that the seat next to her was unoccupied she might even have imagined that all she had to do was turn her head and he'd be there, right beside her. And even though it was utterly ridiculous, she still had to drag her gaze away from the window to quickly check, just to convince herself she *was* alone.

What she saw made her suck in her breath. There might have been hundreds of miles of empty space below her, but the empty space beside her was now taken up by a brawny bearded man with wild dark hair.

'Ryan! What the heck?'

The black beard was split by a glint of white teeth as he grinned at her.

'You were sparko, I wondered when you'd wake up.'

'Jeez!' Chloe looked away in case she was hallucinating. When she looked back he was still there; six-foot-four of pirate raider, ready to assail her brittle defences.

'I nearly missed the flight,' he explained, 'but they were very good when I checked in and even upgraded me.'

How bloody nice for some, Chloe fumed. Naturally, Ryan *would* be upgraded. All those lovely stewardesses were probably thrilled to bits to have an excuse to pay special attention to such a wickedly handsome man. Well, he wasn't going to overwhelm *her*. Sneaking up on her whilst she was asleep might have given him the advantage of surprise, but he was mistaken if he thought she was about to surrender to his buccaneering charms. Especially after three months without so much as a postcard from one of those wilderness places he relished so much.

'Ryan,' she managed to say, despite her clenched jaw. 'What are you doing here?'

'It's fine. Don't worry, I okayed it before I swapped. I'd almost forgotten how little leg room you get in the cheap seats though,' he added, spreading himself out. 'Good job there are people like you who don't need much space, eh?'

'Ryan!' This time her reply came out as a roar.

'Is everything all right, sir?' a passing stewardess asked, giving Chloe the evil eye.

'My friend here's a little worried about landing,' Ryan said, waving her away, and giving Chloe's hand a reassuring pat at the same time. 'But don't worry, I'll look after her and see that she doesn't make a scene.'

Excessively groomed eyebrows rose in a manner that suggested that Chloe didn't realise how lucky she was. Chloe let it wash over her; she had a much bigger bone to pick. If Ryan imagined he could avoid a scene he had another think coming.

'So, what *are* you doing here?' she repeated, quietly.

'Look,' he said quickly, squeezing her hand, 'I know this isn't what you were expecting — '

'Ha! That's a bit of an understatement! Remember, it was *you* who told me to go off and see the world before I went back to everyday life and *you* who encouraged me to explore on my own.'

Her last glimpse of him in the rear-view mirror of her car, after their rose-tinted summer affair, had been through a mist of tears and a dust-cloud of sand as the tyres rolled over a rough track baked hard by the heat. And every morning she had woken up alone in the weeks since then had grown a little colder.

'And *you* asked me not to forget you,' he said, watching her carefully. 'That's why I'm here, because I couldn't get you out of my head. I've thought about you every day since you left.'

'Hmm.' It was a lot to take in. 'Well, you certainly managed to keep those thoughts to yourself. You didn't even get in touch to see if I was home safely.'

'That was a bit difficult when I didn't have your number.'

'Oh.' Thinking back, Chloe remembered there'd been no need to worry about phone numbers because they'd spent the entire two weeks with each other.

'Also, you'd booked the cottage through a third-party website and you were in the process of looking for a new job and a new place to live.' He shrugged. 'I could have trawled through social media, I guess, but that seemed a bit stalkery. Besides, most people go on holiday for a temporary escape, so when there was no word from you, I wasn't sure if you'd even welcome hearing from me. All I knew for certain was when you'd be flying to Hong Kong because I helped you make the booking. And that knowledge was driving me crazy because it was my one shot at seeing you again. I knew if I didn't act I'd always be left wondering about where you were and what you were doing . . . so here I am.'

Chloe wilted as her shock and anger at being so wrong-footed was displaced by a fluttering sense of hope. What if she'd walked away too quickly? Sometimes she was her own worst enemy, spotting potential disasters where there were none and always playing safe. Perhaps this was a moment of self-revelation for both her *and* Ryan; by taking off on a solo holiday — even if it did happen to offer a neat bridge between her past and her future — she'd proved to herself she could loosen up if she wanted to.

As for Ryan? Maybe Ryan had decided that a little more commitment on his part didn't mean she was about to rush off and take out an immediate subscription to *Wedding* magazine. She looked up at him, daring to believe that something wonderful was about to happen. Then he spoke and spoilt the moment.

'I'm going to be left with a lot of egg on my face, if I've got this wrong, but we had fun together, didn't we? But it was over too quickly. And it seems to me that this is a great opportunity to get to know each other better, if that's what you'd like. Who knows? Maybe I haven't got what it takes to be your forever man, but I could be your 'just for now' man if you're willing to take that chance.'

Just for now? And risk getting in even deeper? She squeezed her eyes shut so as not to be influenced by his dark eyes looking at her so beseechingly, but that only made her more aware of the warmth of his thumb sliding over the back of her hand. The small, sensuous circles he was tracing reminded her of all the pleasure those clever fingers were capable of giving. She liked his hands, so strong and sexy, so deft. So good with a camera. Her eyes snapped open. 'Just tell me one thing.'

'Anything,' he said, smiling.

'Is this a working holiday for you?'

The smile faded a little. 'Hong Kong's such an exciting city you never know what you'll see. You couldn't expect me not to bring a camera, could you?'

'Then you'll understand if I don't rush to take you up on your offer.'

There was her answer. Confirmation, as if she needed it, of why Ryan Green would always be Mr Wrong. That square of glass he put between himself and the world was what won him awards for being such a brilliant photographer. It also kept him at a distance and stopped him getting truly involved, as if the beautiful, evocative images he was famous for came at the cost of a sliver of ice in his heart.

'‘Just for now' sounds like work with benefits, because you made it abundantly clear that you'll always put work first,' Chloe continued, quickly pulling herself together. 'Only, I'm not sure what the benefit is to me . . . apart from the fleeting pleasure of your company, I suppose, before you disappear in pursuit of the next shoot.' She shook her head. 'You can't just turn up out of the blue and expect me to slot in with your plans. You're not even supposed to be here, remember? As it happens, I've got some research of my own to do. I've made a list of places I want to see and I'll visit as many as I can pack in.'

He gave a short laugh. 'Top ten sights you must see in Hong Kong, I suppose! Look, don't worry about all that stuff, I could take you to places you'd never dream of.'

That was the problem, Chloe thought unhappily, and then you woke up.

'Funnily enough,' she broke in quickly, 'that's exactly what I'm working on.'

'Oh?' He cocked his head.

'Yes.' She nodded. 'I've got a new job since I saw you. I've moved from local radio; I'm starting work as a researcher for a national show so I'll be doing some research for a special travel feature while I'm away.'

'Well that's great news,' he said with a disarming flash of teeth through the dense beard. 'Congratulations! It was high time you were given the opportunity to do some real research instead of running around making the tea for that oily ex of yours. Ha! I bet he's sorry to lose you.'

Chloe shifted, suddenly uncomfortable in the confined space.

'Hmm, actually I'm going with him. It was Guy who offered me the job.'

Ryan winced. 'You cannot be serious! Nothing you've ever said about him suggests he'll let you develop your career; you'll be too busy running errands for him.'

'No. That'll be someone else's job,' Chloe insisted. 'I'll be finding stories, contributors and coming up with ideas. This is a great opportunity for me.'

'I really hope so.' Ryan went quiet then added, 'I can't believe you're abandoning Wilma for that toad!'

'Who said anything about abandoning Wilma?' Chloe glared at him. 'She's coming with me.'

'Right, right.' Ryan chuckled to himself. 'That'll go well then. Have you forgotten all that stuff you told me about him? Isn't this the same man who wanted you to choose between him and Wilma last time? If you're giving him a second chance, you'd better make sure he takes out some good house contents cover because those cream carpets you told me about are going to take a hit. Oh, and if he can lose his sense of smell, so much that better, especially once Wilma forgets her manners.'

Chloe folded her arms and thought

about asking if *he'd* lost his sense of hearing. What part of 'new job' hadn't he heard? As for jumping to the conclusion that she was moving in with Guy, well that was actually rather insulting. Hadn't he learned anything about her during the time they'd been together? She thought about it. It was true that Ryan had been very tolerant of Wilma's lack of inhibitions and he'd been great when she'd eaten one of his favourite boots. And then chewed a shoe for dessert. Mostly because he was too busy staring at the newest images for his current project to even notice.

'Ryan, none of this is anything you need worry about, remember? All I'm doing is getting on with my life.'

'Okaaaay.' Ryan placed his other hand on top of hers and gave it another little pat before letting go completely. 'Well, if that's what you want, I'm happy for you.'

Chloe acknowledged him with a nod. 'It's strange how things work out,' she added after a short pause. 'I needed a break; Hong Kong's been on my bucket list of places to visit for years but I would never have got round to booking it without you.'

He perked up immediately. 'Exactly! Which is why it seemed such a fun thing to do together. To be with you. To see all the places I love through your eyes. We should live in the moment; life's too short to sit around agonising about every decision.'

He wasn't wrong about that, thought Chloe. Life *could* be short but that wasn't a good reason to behave recklessly. Some people were fragile, easily broken, and she had no intention of getting hurt again. 'I'm grateful to you as a friend, but I don't need a 'just for now man',' she said, firmly.

He heaved a sigh. 'I'm sorry, that was crass of me. I can see that I should have thought this through properly. I should have realised that you were in the process of clearing your head when you were staying in Little Spitmarsh . . . I guess I hadn't anticipated that you were going home to more of the same.'

'Wanting stability is not 'more of the same,'' she insisted. 'I've had enough of change. I'm not like you, I don't like not knowing what's round the corner. I'm sorry if that sounds dull.'

'You could never be dull,' he said, shaking his head.

Chloe turned away to hide the sudden tears that were pricking her eyes. For a moment they sat there listening to the hum of the engine and the hiss of air conditioning, then Ryan laid his hand on her arm.

'Okay, I realise I've completely misjudged the situation, but at least let me try to salvage something. Since we're both going to be in the same city and I'm in position to help you with your research, can't we at least spend some time together?

Chloe opened her mouth to speak but he anticipated her. 'As friends,' he said with a sad smile that went through her.

She nodded, not trusting herself to

speak in case a tremor in her voice betrayed how much she wished it could be different between them. *Friends.* She tried it out in her head. *My friend, Ryan.* Again. *My friend, Ryan, who makes me laugh, makes me cry, has the sexiest smile and a body made to give a girl hours of endless pleasure.* Deep breath. Not. Too. Bad. Okay, she could do this. Then she glanced up at her new friend, saw the thick dark lashes flutter as he closed his eyes and ached all over again.

3

'Yes' was such a little word, not difficult to say at all, Ryan concluded as they left the sleek, air-conditioned terminal and stepped out into warm sunshine. If only he'd used it instead of prevaricating when Chloe invited him to accompany her to her dad's wedding, he wouldn't be bracing himself for a week of pretending to be friends now. He watched her dark head disappear as she slid into the back seat of the taxi and reminded himself to smile when he walked round to the other side and joined her.

Nothing he'd ever heard about or from Chloe's ex — curiosity had got the better of him, forcing him to track down and listen to a couple of clips from his radio show — suggested that he was anything else but a mollusc so the thought of him sliming his way back

32

into her affections was killing him. Worse still, Ryan knew he only had himself to blame; if only he'd tried harder to track her down before gate-crashing her solo trip. If only he'd thought twice before opening his mouth and frightening her off with his 'here and now, live for the moment' philosophy.

'How's that working out for you?' he could imagine his cousin, Tansy asking, her sharp voice ringing out in his head. 'Isn't that the kind of woman you're looking for? Someone independent and free-spirited, you said.'

He could still see the expression on Tansy's face when he'd asked her to mind Fred, his beloved basset hound. That barely suppressed grin when he outlined all the good, practical reasons why he'd moved heaven and earth to book a trip to Hong Kong at the same time as Chloe.

'Practical. Of course,' she'd agreed. 'After all, a relationship with any woman who can't cope with you pursuing your own interests is a non-starter, isn't it? Like Katie, that investment banker, remember? The one you met at an exhibition? Said she was a huge admirer of your work.'

'It turned out that her artistic admiration only stretched so far,' Ryan granted. It certainly didn't extend to letting him actually get on with his work. Every time he had to go away for a shoot, she bent his ear about being abandoned.

'At least you didn't have that problem with Gabriella, that model who was always going on about your 'sexy dark looks'.'

'So I could play the dumb supporting role, providing her with a decorative arm to hang off at social functions whilst she flirted with other men's cameras.' The hissy fits when the unpredictable nature of his work left her without an escort at the last minute, only made him more inclined to stay away for as long as possible. 'Frankly, it was a relief when she left me for that racing driver. The thing is, Tans, any woman who wants to get involved with me must understand that my work comes first.'

'*Lovely.* Just what every girl wants to hear,' Tansy said with sarcastic emphasis.

Ignoring her, Ryan kissed her on the cheek then crouched down to say goodbye to Fred.

'That's why you're hell-bent on going all the way to Hong Kong with Chloe, is it?' Tansy went on. 'To tell her that your work comes first? I'm sure she'll be delighted when she finds out.'

As Ryan stood up, she caught hold of his arm. 'Ryan, what happened to your dad wasn't just bad luck. He pushed himself too hard and ignored the warning signs. You've always been fitter and more laid back. You're not the same as him. That's really what this is about, isn't it?'

'I wouldn't wish what Ma and Pa have been through on anyone,' he said, quietly. 'One moment it was all going swimmingly for them; a good life, lovely holidays, plans for the future and the next? Well, you know what an uphill struggle it's been for them since Pa's stroke. But this isn't anything to do with him. No one knows what the future holds which is why my only plan is to make the most of today.'

His plan, it seemed, needed work. Far from being delighted by his spontaneity, Chloe seemed pretty determined to stick to her own agenda. No wonder the look she gave him, as he dropped in beside her, spoke volumes.

'It's about half an hour's drive to Mong Kok and your hotel; you might as well sit back and enjoy the view.'

She threw him a quick smile, at last. She'd refreshed her signature Rouge Allure lipstick before landing and it made him nostalgic for the nights when he'd found it in all kinds of interesting places. *Forget it*, he reminded himself, staring blankly out of the taxi window as they left the airport behind. The problem was he'd assumed that given the speed at which their affair had progressed, she was as relaxed and carefree about it as he was. It was only after she'd walked away that he worked out how much of herself she'd given to him to let her guard down so completely. Big mistake. So if the only chance he had of getting back into her life was to be the best friend she ever had, the brother she'd never had, or even just a shoulder to lean on, well, hell, that idea completely sucked.

When she turned to him, her fine dark hair fanning out from her face, her brown eyes shining with excitement, he itched to pick up his camera, frame the shot and capture the pure wonder of her expression.

'You know, there was that moment when I realised I was actually flying over the South China Sea when I had almost had to pinch myself to convince myself it was really happening, but look, I'm really here! I imagined all these skyscrapers but not the washing strung out from every window. How else would eight million people dry their laundry when space is at such a premium?'

'You're impressed by the laundry?' He laughed.

'You know what I mean; it's that sense of the familiar being unfamiliar — of being somewhere different. I can't wait to get out and explore.'

'You might want to remember that washing when we do; avoid the drips, is my advice.' *Same applies to men*, he nearly added. He pointed to the glass-fronted building where the taxi was slowing down. 'This is us — we're here.'

She hadn't baulked at his casual 'we' when he spoke about exploring, but the sight of the hotel had made her go quiet and she was wearing *The Look* again; defensive and dejected at the same time.

'Same hotel, different room, of course,' he assured her quickly before they checked in. 'With hindsight maybe even booking the same place wasn't such a great idea either, but look, we've both got to eat this evening; it seems crazy not to dine together. How about we take the easy option and see what's on the hotel's menu tonight?'

'No, I don't think so,' she said, diving on her key card so as to catch up with an eager porter who was bearing her bag towards the lifts. 'But thanks for the offer. I think I'll just have a shower and head off to take a look around.'

'Really?' Ryan frowned at her. 'I mean, it's perfectly safe, but do you really want to wander around all by yourself the first night in a strange city?'

There was a 'ping' and the lift doors slid open. She stepped in and turned to face him. 'Tell me, Ryan,' she said, lifting her chin, 'has anyone ever put that question to you?'

'Fair point,' he admitted as the doors closed again and he found himself staring at a blank black wall of etched glass. 'Just be careful, won't you?'

*   *   *

Even the air smelled different, Chloe noticed as she stepped outside later, a bit like how she imagined the first smell of land would be after a long time at sea. A musky, musty slightly spicy infusion with a faint hint of sewer which quickly permeated her clothes and hair and reminded her she was far from home.

'Hong Kong? Seriously? I thought you hated big cities — wasn't that why you didn't bite my hand off to accept my job offer?'

Guy's voice, ringing in her head as she dried herself after her shower, had almost stopped her leaving her room. Just staring out at the view, the misty blue of the harbour threaded between the glittering skyscrapers and the cluster of apartments glowing copper in the evening light, well that was enough of an experience in itself, wasn't it?

Of course, telling Guy that she wasn't keen to move to London was simply a way of buying time while she weighed up her options. Seemingly oblivious to her real concern, he'd immediately upped the salary offer, which was a nice bonus, but was it even possible to work alongside the man she'd had a two-year relationship with?

'It's really inconvenient; I was relying on you to get on with the grunt work so that I can hit the ground running,' he'd grumbled when she explained why she couldn't simply drop everything to rush to his side. 'I mean Hong Kong — what were you thinking of? I guarantee you'll hate it. Your sense of direction's hopeless, you're too squeamish by half and designer brands and shopping malls bore you silly. Really, Chloe, I could have saved you an awful lot of money if you'd told me you were booking a holiday. The Balearics are so much more you; sandy beaches, sunshine, plenty of nightlife . . . I might even have been able to have taken some time off myself. Although maybe it would have been a bit soon . . . '

'For what?' she'd shot back, smarting at the idea that she came across as the kind of person looking for a rave mecca and a sun-bed by the pool to sleep off her hangover the next day. 'Guy, I accepted the job for professional reasons, remember?'

And that was where it would stay, Chloe resolved, recalling how Guy's prime concerns were always for himself. Unimaginable now to think this was the man who'd broken her heart. Whose behaviour hurt her so much she'd had to slink off to an unfashionable seaside resort to lick her wounds and where, that memorable summer night, she'd been rudely introduced to Ryan when his basset hound had thundered up to Wilma with dishonourable intentions. After that, she certainly hadn't thought very much about Guy during the two most wonderful, fun-packed weeks of her life.

However, the prospect of embarking on a new professional relationship with her ex-boyfriend and boss was certainly making her think about him now. It suited him to have her there to do the donkey work while he concentrated on building his audience, but unless she proved herself quickly and stepped out from Guy's shadow at an early stage, she'd be forever stuck on the bottom rung of the career ladder.

Telling Ryan she had research to do might have been stretching the truth, but why not return from her holiday with a ready-made programme feature? Everyone loved to dream about their holidays, didn't they? So instead of letting Guy run away with the idea that she was a soft touch, only there to do his bidding, she'd show him she could be innovative and independent-minded too. Especially after he'd stooped to the most underhand tactics to discourage her from travelling.

'I do remember that your food tastes are distinctly unadventurous,' he'd taunted. 'You'll struggle with that in Hong Kong with its 'waste not, want not' cuisine. Make sure you know what you're biting into first or you might find it's something you definitely don't want to chew.'

At least she could spot a snake when she saw one. Guy had taught her that much when he'd tried to make her choose between him and her adorable little dachshund, Wilma. Chloe had opted for the choice with the short legs and long body even though Wilma's flatulence was much worse than Guy's. And look what had happened next. Now, she was finished with Guy *and* Ryan. In fact, she was finished with all men. Even her dad, depending on whether or not he carried on behaving like a lovesick teenager *after* his wedding, was on the critical list.

Of all the unwelcome thoughts swirling around in her head, it was those she was most determined to avoid that gave her the push she needed to leave the hotel. Now she was rather pleased with herself for making the move. *Number One from your new travel correspondent*, she thought, her mind racing ahead, *Eating Out in Hong Kong*.

After the dreary wet autumn she'd

left behind, the evening was pleasantly warm; perfect T-shirt weather. And although she was initially wary in case she inadvertently offended some local custom, she soon discovered that everyone was too busy minding their own business to worry in the slightest about her.

The local restaurants were, however, bafflingly Chinese — *well, duh, Chloe, what else were they going to be?* And some of the street food was a little too heavy in beaks, feet and heads for her taste so she carried on walking looking for a less challenging option. Having taken a long detour to what seemed to be Car Repair Street in one direction and Sink and Tap Street in another, she was beginning to feel quite weary so retraced her footsteps and picked the most inviting looking restaurant which, she quickly realised once inside, was a little . . . basic.

Bored men, slurping bowls of noodles as they watched a flickering telly, glanced up in dull surprise as an unsmiling waitress ushered her to a Formica-topped table and waved an illustrated menu with English subtitles only briefly under her nose before whisking it away.

'Good,' said the waitress, jabbing her finger at a photo of something that looked like crispy duck. Coincidentally, Chloe noticed it also happened to be the most expensive item on the menu. Okay, the subtitle also claimed that it was goose, but, what the heck, she was too tired to complain. Crispy duck, crispy goose? Whatever. And something to go with it; some carbs and a few veg. Chloe pointed to dishes of noodles, green beans and then, feeling very proud of herself as the waitress's severe features were softened by a look of admiration, managed to signal that she'd like a beer as well. Goodness, how she needed the beer! When the goose arrived along with a couple of interested staff to tell her how 'good!' it was and watch her take her first mouthfuls, Chloe panicked. The sight of a whole bird stretched out on a serving dish, rather like an ancient sunbather with its tanned leathery skin, immediately made her lose her appetite. It wasn't the tiny portion she'd anticipated, but enough to feed everyone in the restaurant. Once massive bowls of noodles and green beans were also set down in front of her, she found herself trembling at the foot of a food mountain. How on earth was she going to get through it all? Putting on a brave face so as not to offend the staff who were so keen for her to enjoy her meal, she was seriously contemplating a fake faint into her noodles when someone slid across the table opposite her.

'I presume this seat isn't taken?' Ryan said, grinning at her. 'Although you've ordered enough to feed an army.'

'Ryan! Thank God! Help me, will you?'

★   ★   ★

'Next time,' he said later, having gamely chewed his way through the greater part of a goose, the huge plate of noodles and a fair share of beans, 'maybe you'll let me help when you're looking for a place to eat?'

Chloe's heart went out to him; he was so lovely, so gallant, picking out the best bits of meat and giving them to her, making her laugh with his stories about the weirdest foods he'd ever eaten, making the evening fun. Something about Ryan made everything better and brighter. And it was so lucky that he happened to be there, just when she needed him.

'I know a really great dim sum restaurant,' he said, leaning across the table.

'Great,' she said, reaching in her handbag for her purse. 'Let me know if it's as good as you remember and I might give it a try.'

'I thought we could go there tomorrow,' he said, frowning.

Tomorrow? That was commitment from a man who would almost certainly abandon her in a heartbeat if a sudden photographic opportunity presented itself. She looked at him, his hirsute good looks and broad shoulders accentuated by the black T-shirt he was wearing, and hurt all over again

'And tonight?' she asked quietly. 'Still working on the 'just for now' plan? From table talk to pillow talk, is that what you were thinking? Is that why you followed me this evening?'

He didn't speak for a minute. She was about to get up when he reached across the table and took her hand before she had a chance to pull away.

'Chloe, it's your first night in a strange city. When I spotted you earlier wandering off in the opposite direction to the restaurants, I went after you to make sure you were safe,' he said and gave her an apologetic smile. 'Maybe I should have owned up sooner. I wasn't stalking you I was simply looking out for you as a friend.'

She shook her head. Trying to be friends with the man she still ached for was just too painful. 'Thank you,' she said, withdrawing her hand and getting up, 'but as much as I appreciate you wading in to help me avert a possible diplomatic incident tonight, I am capable of looking after myself, you know? Oh, and you've got noodle in your beard.'

Ryan nodded, dabbed his chin and gave her a wry smile. 'Looks as if I cooked my goose, saving you from yours.'

A memory of seeing that disarming smile first thing in the morning momentarily unsettled her, but Chloe congratulated herself for staying strong. Even with noodles in his beard, Ryan still had the power to make her heart beat faster. Raging physical attraction was all very well, but what Chloe wanted most was a lasting relationship, and Ryan could never give her the security she craved. That was reason enough, she decided, to get used to exploring on her own. Over breakfast, she'd draw up a list of 'must dos' and tick off as many as she could, beginning with something easy like some window shopping and a trip to Kowloon Park. What wasn't to like about a walk in the park?

4

Number one on her 'must do' list, 'Sample the Local Cuisine', hadn't got off to the best start, Chloe decided the next morning, but she was bound to come across something delicious whilst ticking off number two, 'Soak up the Local Culture'. Under walls of glass in the hotel lobby she wavered, caught for a moment between a simple human desire for some company and a need to prove to herself that she'd be fine on her own. Then she pulled herself together and took a step forward.

'Wait a minute!'

Chloe hurried on. Outside, the streets were already bustling; crouched at the feet of soaring buildings, sharp-eyed vendors waited for trade in open-front shops where toilet rolls jostled for space besides spring onions and skeins of dried sausages swung from hooks and baked in the warm air.

'Go away,' she told Ryan as he caught up with her.

'I'm not running after you for the exercise,' Ryan said with a slow smile that still made her knees weak. 'I have a proposal.'

'Oh, yes?' Chloe said, lifting an eyebrow. 'Then show me the ring.'

The smile disappeared. Ryan went pale and stopped dead.

'It's all right, 'Mr Just for Now', I was only teasing.' Chloe shook her head and went on alone, but it was only a temporary pause while Ryan gathered himself and picked up the pace again.

'Photos.'

He sounded smug, but Chloe, wilting in the heat, had just spotted the cool sanctuary of the nearest MTR station. Adding 'Easy Ways to Get About' to her mental checklist, she headed down the escalator.

'A picture's worth a thousand words,' Ryan said, bending his head to her ear as he caught up with her. 'Think how much better your presentation will look with some first-class images.'

'It's a radio show,' Chloe pointed out, jerking round and almost smacking her mouth against his. She spun back immediately, but not before she'd seen the gleam of heat in his grey eyes. Trying to hang on to her self-control when she knew what that flash of heat meant was a lot harder than she thought. What part of her imagined that a week of pretending to be friends with Ryan would somehow erase the memories of all that warmth, his hot mouth on hers, his body moving against hers? Shaking her head, she scanned the information boards and picked a platform.

'With its own website, naturally,' he said, still following her. 'Of course *you* can take snaps, but *I'm* the professional.'

Oh, he was very good at all kinds of things, Chloe thought, eyeing his reflection in the dark glass, as he stood behind her waiting. Now he'd added a new skill, that of turning up when she least expected him and throwing her into total confusion. And Chloe hated confusion; it made her insecure and miserable. Confusion turned things upside down when she liked to stay in control of what was going on. Being organised and well-prepared meant she was ready when the inevitable Bad Things came along and her systematic approach made her a good researcher. Some people — Ryan — liked to throw caution to the wind, but being dependable would prove to Guy that she was someone he could count on.

She started to consider Ryan's suggestion as they boarded a train where exquisite girls and sleek boys, straight out the pages of *Vogue*, were glossy with head-to-toe designer labels and busily scanning their phones. They, like the lavish shopping malls above them when Chloe and Ryan emerged again, reflected another aspect of Hong Kong's complex personality. In what felt like miles of jewellery shops, there was a brisk trade in eye-wateringly expensive diamond rings and luxury watches. Cameras, handbags, designer clothes were everywhere in the busy modern city with its huge appetite for the new and costly, something Guy, who had tried so hard to put her off, would have applauded.

Kowloon Park was an oasis of tranquility amongst the hustle and bustle of the big city. Sitting by one of the large fountains enjoying the sight of fluting birds hiding in the trees and exotic butterflies drinking from hibiscus, Chloe was enchanted by a cluster of adorable tiny school children beetling towards them like little ladybirds with their identical red rucksacks strapped to their backs.

'Watch this,' said Ryan.

Chloe hoped that her expression wasn't too hungry or too filled with longing as she did what she was told. It was something of a mixed blessing to be given an excuse for an unashamed ogle. He was lovely to look at but much too flighty to risk falling for all over again. Nevertheless, she couldn't drag her eyes away as he ambled towards the group, who turned as one with an air of apprehension which melted away when he smiled and greeted them. A teacher, one of three accompanying the children, covered her mouth with her hand and cast coy looks at the large bearded man as he explained something to her. She, in turn, bent to have a word with her small pupils who all waved and chorused 'hellos' as if they'd been joined by a most honoured visitor. Whilst enthralling his small audience with conjuring tricks, pulling coins from the air and sending little origami birds into flight Ryan managed, at the same time, to take photos of their enchanted faces. How easy it was for him to charm his subjects.

The previews, when he returned and showed them to Chloe, captured the moment in a way that she knew was completely beyond her. No one could resist Ryan's magic; it had almost worked on her last night as he gazed across the table, mesmerising her with the full spotlight of his attention. Until, of course, it was time for the next frame when you were shoved into the shadows. Yes, the disappearing trick was something he excelled at. All she had to do was remind herself that behind the candid, revealing photographs was an objective mind and a cold clear eye.

'All right, you've made your point,' she admitted. 'How much?'

Ryan tipped his head on one side, considering. 'My usual rates might be too expensive for you, I'm afraid.'

'Then what?' Why make the suggestion if he knew she couldn't afford it? She glanced across at him and he gave a slow smile in return, the twinkle in his eye making her pulse race.

'A thousand words.'

A butterfly landed on her knee. Ryan's camera clicked before she could blink.

'I'll give you ten photographs to use as you wish,' he went on, 'but, of course, I'll be making my own record of the trip and I'll be sending my photographs to an agency. With a feature article written by you to accompany the pictures, they'll be especially attractive to travel magazines and websites.'

Chloe blew her fringe off her forehead. 'But I've never done anything like that before.'

'So?' he said, getting up. 'Are you a researcher or not? Time to talk the talk; if you can't put something interesting together in a thousand words, you'd better go back to making the tea for your boss.'

★ ★ ★

Two days later, Ryan was beginning to think his plan had backfired on him. Chloe had simply acknowledged they'd accomplish more of her goals if they worked together and handed the camera work entirely over to him while they ticked off her list of places she wanted to visit. The only indication of the intimacy they had once relished was a worried frown from Chloe — like now as he touched a hand lightly to her shoulder — whenever he got too near. She looked away, her gaze flicking to the traffic signal as it began to beep frantically, hurrying them across.

'Wow! Look at that! Is that really bamboo scaffolding?' She stopped to lean back and take a good look at the construction work on the tower block soaring high above them.

'Uh-huh.' As a man pushing a trolley loaded with timber came towards them, Ryan moved out of the way so that he was close enough to Chloe to feel the heat of her body and smell the sweet scent of her perfume rising from her hair. He scratched his head, frustrated that she was more interested in scaffolding than him. 'They're much cheaper than metal poles,' he explained, wondering if impressing her with his knowledge of the city would cut him any slack. 'Skilled scaffolders here can rig up to a thousand feet of scaffolding a day, but it's not work for the faint-hearted.'

'And not something Health and Safety back home would approve of,' she nodded. 'Amazing! Can you get some pictures of it to add to the portfolio? Guy ought to be seriously impressed when he sees what I've come back with,' she added with some satisfaction.

Something unwelcome and unfamiliar thumped through Ryan's chest. Jealousy. Somewhere deep inside it stung that he was going out of his way to help her with a project that would probably make her even more attractive to Guy. Not cool, Ryan, he reminded himself thinking how much he despised that sense of ownership when he saw it in other men. He had no right to feel possessive about Chloe so why did he resent her eagerness to please another man? If there wasn't something in Chloe's expression, a look from the corner of her eye, that she gave him when she thought he wasn't looking, he'd give up now. Rip the memory card from his camera, drop it in in her hands and walk away. Just like that. Except that the mistiness in her eyes, the way her soft mouth lifted in a quick smile when she saw him for the first time each day and the sheer nakedness of her unguarded emotions still gave him hope that he could be more to her than just a friend.

They turned the corner where the air was thick with the scent of lilies and roses and a small lady in a wide-brimmed straw hat tended plastic buckets of wrapped flowers spilling out across the pavement so that pedestrians had to squeeze by.

'The Flower Market,' he said, unnecessarily. 'Orchids,' he went, on pointing at serried ranks in shades from deepest purple to purest white, 'are a symbol of nobility here, as well as just being beautiful. Bamboo, as you probably know, is used a lot in feng shui, it's supposed to create a happy home. It's pretty easy to care for too.'

'That's about all it's got going for it,' Chloe said. 'But maybe I'll get one for my new flat anyway.'

If the new flat turned out to be anything to do with Guy, Ryan wished for the bamboo to shrivel up and wilt.

'Exciting times, then,' he forced himself to say as they wandered to the nearby Bird Garden, 'new job, new home. Seems that your future's all mapped out.'

Above them the air chimed with the trills and warbles of birdsong. This was where, in a long tradition, owners competed to see whose caged pet birds had the most beautiful repertoire. Ryan started to take a few pictures.

'Some of those cages are really small,' he heard Chloe say unhappily.

'It's probably safer for the birds in this situation,' he replied, looking back at her. 'They're very highly prized by their owners so they certainly don't want them to come to any harm. They're brought outside for fresh air and sunshine, not just to show them off. Bird walking's firmly established in the culture of this place.'

Chloe shook her head, 'I'd rather see a beautiful creature flying free. I thought about putting Wilma in kennels when I came away, but it just wasn't an option. I know she'd be well cared for, but she wouldn't understand. I couldn't bear the thought of her being scared or worrying that she'd been abandoned. She'll be much happier with Dad in her own environment. The only danger there is that he'll spoil her rotten.'

'It's going to be difficult for her when she finds herself in a strange flat all day,' Ryan couldn't help but point out.

'It's not ideal,' she admitted quietly, her gaze darting back to the cages. 'It's the moving part I'm most worried about really . . . '

'Perhaps you might have to think about leaving Wilma with your father on a semi-permanent basis? I know it's easy for me to say that when my cousin, Tansy's only round the corner. She's always willing take Fred at short notice on the rare occasions when he can't accompany me and it gives me peace of mind to know that he's safe and happy with her.'

She shot him an agonised look.

'Or she could stay with me until you're sure this job's going to work out. Fred and I are very fond of her,' he added, thinking aloud.

'It *will* work out,' Chloe said, firmly. 'I'm not going to pretend it will be easy, but Wilma's home is with me. I'm not giving up on this career opportunity before I've even started. Whatever differences there have been between me and Guy in the past, he's really good at his job. He might be working the graveyard shift to begin with, but when his new bosses see his audience appeal he'll soon get a primetime slot. I want to make sure that I'm the researcher he takes with him.'

'You wouldn't have been offered the job in the first place unless you had the skills and experience to do it,' he said, frowning at her over his camera. Unless her ex had an ulterior motive for wanting Chloe to be by his side. He shifted his gaze to Chloe's back as she walked away, taking in the neat curve of her waist, the gentle sway of her hips beneath the white linen skirt and admitted he couldn't blame Guy. The graveyard shift and the dead hours of the night would always come to life when Chloe was around. The first thing he'd noticed when Chloe exited his life was how long the nights were without her. How still the house was when it was just him. And Fred, of course, although even Fred kept looking at the dachshund-shaped space in his dog bed left by Wilma and turning back to Ryan with a sad, recriminatory expression.

'I admit it would be convenient for Guy if I picked up where I left off,' she allowed as he caught up with her. 'I make his job easier for him,' she continued, 'I know exactly how he likes his coffee, what time to bring it. I know he hates mess, so I keep the studio tidy. I know which guests to welcome and which to fend off . . . '

'It sounds more like a tired marriage

than a working relationship,' Ryan couldn't stop himself saying.

'Except, this is a new start,' Chloe said with a bright smile that didn't reach her eyes. 'Which is why I'm going to be proactive about work so that it's my research and organisation skills Guy notices rather than whether or not I've tracked down the right sandwich for him when he's peckish.'

'You know, the more I hear about this man, the more I dislike him,' Ryan said, thoroughly annoyed. 'Are you sure *you* won't be walking into a gilded cage, dancing to Guy's tune?'

At least *he'd* never sent Chloe out to buy his sandwiches. In fact, he'd made a point of showing off his cooking skills, making all kinds of delicacies for her and even bringing her smoked salmon and scrambled eggs and a glass of bubbly for breakfast one morning. The flash of anger was banished by a warmer feeling as he remembered how he'd brought up her tray dressed only in a navy apron folded and tied round his middle. Chloe had sat up naked in the rumpled bed all tousled with sleep, and giggled as he came round to join her. They'd only got as far as raising their glasses in a toast and taking a sip when suddenly neither of them seemed that hungry.

'The thing is,' Chloe said, fishing in her bag for her sunglasses. 'Guy was prepared to take me on when I was a complete novice, when no one else would give me a chance.'

'Why do you say that?' He ducked out the way of a low-hanging bird cage, one of the last in the line.

She hesitated for a moment before replying. 'I'd just started at university when my mum died. She hadn't been well for a while, but her death was still a terrible shock. The knock-on effect on my exams rather put pay to my studies, but I didn't have the heart to continue with my degree by then. Suddenly it just didn't seem to matter any more.'

'I'm so sorry, Chloe, that must have been a horrible time for you. How tragic,' he said, wishing he could pull her to him and comfort her.

'It wasn't all bad,' she insisted, although the slight tremor in her voice, suggested otherwise. 'I did some voluntary work for the local hospital radio which led to Guy taking me on as his researcher. It also meant I didn't have to leave home so I was there for Dad when he needed me most.'

Ryan was trying to process everything Chloe had told him when he noticed they were passing the Goldfish Market. Guessing what Chloe's reaction was likely to be, he tried to hurry her past the rows and rows of plastic bags glittering so attractively in the sunshine.

'What's in the — ?'

He watched the expectant smile fade as she peered at the hundreds of live exotic fish of all shapes and sizes crammed into dozens of bags hung out to attract passing trade.

'They're just temporary homes,' Ryan told her quickly. 'Goldfish represent wealth in feng shui, so when someone buys a bagged fish, they're taking their bag of gold home.'

'Assuming the poor things last that long,' Chloe muttered, backing away.

Ryan saw her blink and slide a hand across her cheek. He was pretty sure that a man like Guy had every intention of using Chloe to enrich his own position. It seemed to him that the shock of losing her mother had robbed Chloe of her freedom, trapping her in her professional life with a man who had taken advantage of her when she was at her lowest point.

Gripped by frustration that there seemed to be nothing he could do to make Chloe aware that she was walking into what he was afraid was a dead-end street, Ryan put his mind to addressing how best to spend their last two days together. Whatever happened in the future, he wanted only to create happy memories for Chloe of her holiday in Hong Kong. Then inspiration struck. 'It's your call,' he said, spotting a stall where they could sit down and have a

cold drink out of the sun, 'but I have a
suggestion for something you might like
to do tomorrow . . . '

5

Chloe paused to take stock of the vibrant scene before her, delighted that she had put any reservations about Ryan's suggestion aside. With only two days left in this exciting city, she was determined to experience as much of it as possible. And what better way than to do that than with someone who was as familiar with the place as Ryan?

Ryan, quite rightly, was looking rather pleased at what he'd conjured up. If anything was going to bring her research to life it was this extraordinary temple. Vivid red pillars with accents of gleaming gold glowed in the sunlight and a profusion of noisy stalls teeming with customers gave the place the bustling atmosphere of a grand bazaar rather than a shrine.

'It's famous for the many prayers that are supposed to be answered here,' said

Ryan. 'Every wish granted on request. And if you're in any doubt, you can always buy something to help them on their way.' He pointed to the bundles of incense sticks which were particularly in demand, the fragrant smoke from their glowing tips curling into the air. He drew her in to show her one of the shots he'd taken. 'Now, don't tell me you won't be able to write the words to go with this. Good enough for you?'

Not bad at all, she couldn't help think, somewhat distracted by the muscles of his forearms and the subtle shadowing of fine dark hair across his tanned skin. She leaned in and immediately felt her body tingling at his proximity. It was such a struggle not to touch him, to resist the temptation to run her fingers down his arm. But that would be completely unprofessional, wouldn't it? She gave herself a mental ticking off and concentrated on the stunning image he'd captured. Spirals of incense smoke rose up through spherical red and gold lanterns, past the terracotta flying eaves of the altar and towards the soaring white modern skyscrapers as if to touch the windows of everyday lives.

'That's not fair,' she protested. 'A picture like that doesn't need words — the story's all there.'

Ryan nodded, a smile escaping from behind the undergrowth of his beard. 'Not quite. I think it's missing a personal touch, something that would really give readers a sense of how it feels to experience this place. You should really get your fortune told. Now that *would* give your writing authenticity.'

Chloe had a good laugh at his ridiculous suggestion. Why would she do something so out of character? But on the other hand, this was exactly the place to step outside her comfort zone. All too soon she would be back in England, looking out of an unfamiliar window, watching the November rain pattering on the glass and wondering how many layers to wear before joining the rush hour commute. *That* Chloe would never even flick a curious glance at her horoscope, knew that her chances of winning the lottery were one in fourteen million so saved all her two pound coins in a jar instead and merrily set out every Friday the thirteenth without a backwards glance.

The next thing she knew, she was kneeling before the temple altar, self-consciously rattling her fortune sticks in a bamboo tube, as instructed, waiting for a sign. Ready to shrivel up with embarrassment, she was about to beat a retreat, when one of the red-tipped numbered sticks suddenly slid from the bundle. She threw a quick glance at Ryan, watching her behind his camera, who lifted his head, gave her a thumbs up and beckoned her over.

'Twenty-three, lucky for some!' he said, practically rubbing his hands with glee. 'Now all you have to do is pick an expert to interpret the temple's predictions. Ready?'

Chloe took a deep breath of the

fragrant air. 'Why not? It's a load of baloney anyway, so what harm can it do?'

'That's my girl,' Ryan said (inaccurately, she thought). 'It'll make for some fantastic photographs!'

Chloe held up her hand. 'Er, hang on. This isn't a spectator sport. I don't recall inviting you along to have a good laugh at my expense.'

'But you've just said it's a load of baloney!' he protested as she took a tentative step towards the fortune-telling arcade where soothsayers of all varieties were waiting in booths to take her money.

'Yes, and it's my load of baloney, not yours,' she told him. 'You get can get your own fortune told if you're that keen to know what it's all about. One picture and that's it. Understood?'

★ ★ ★

Ryan had to admit that it was a bit of setback that Chloe was apparently determined not to let him eavesdrop on her reading. His camera, however, had the useful knack of enabling him to blend into the background, so he was confident, as Chloe scanned the stalls with a nervous eye, that she would quickly forget he was there. Whatever he overheard, there was bound to be some suitably enigmatic phrase he could use as a lever to persuade her to let her hair down for the last two evenings of their trip.

'No, a little bird is *not* going to tell me,' Chloe said, pointing to a cubicle where a small white bird was being lifted from a bamboo cage so that it could select cards from the pack spread on the wooden table. 'Call me picky,' she sniffed, 'but if I'm really about to discover what fate has in store for me, I'd prefer to hear it from someone who is at least pretending to know what they're doing rather than trust it to a couple of random pecks. Someone I can understand would probably be a good idea too.'

She stopped in front of stall festooned in swathes of red cloth decorated with gold Chinese lettering where annotated posters of palms and faces seemed to meet her approval. A laminated sign proclaimed, 'English Spoken' although this wasn't immediately apparent when Chloe tried to communicate with the woman behind the desk. Ryan glumly decided that this was about to be the shortest and least revealing consultation ever when Chloe's luck improved. The fortune teller proper, who'd returned from whatever fortune tellers did to recharge their psychic energy, dismissed the stall sitter and, in passable English, invited Chloe to a seat in front of him. He had a kind face, Ryan was pleased to see, so he hoped he wouldn't be too plain-speaking or dwell too much on bad news. It would certainly help the dwindling hours of their precious time if, instead, he drew Chloe's attention to the wonders of the tall, dark, bearded man in her immediate future.

'Three hundred dollars,' the fortune teller began, smiling.

Chloe looked in her wallet and, to

her obvious embarrassment found that she only had two hundred. Ryan was about to step in when the fortune teller, leaning over the table, nodded at her.

'Two hundred dollars,' he said, taking her hand. 'What do you want to know?'

'I'd like to know how to further my career?' she asked in a firm voice.

Tell her not to sleep with her new boss, urged Ryan silently.

'Never give up,' the fortune teller proclaimed.

Chloe's small frown suggested that two hundred dollars was quite a lot to pay for being told the bleeding obvious. The fortune teller continued probing her hand with something that looked a lot like a knitting needle and with many a murmuring of 'beautiful' and 'good' and other promising pronouncements. He then indicated that she should lift her hair back from her face. 'Let me see sky,' he said, pointing to his own forehead. Ryan hoped that they were finally going to get to some juicy stuff and was disappointed to hear him tell

Chloe that the good news was that a fresh start was going to be hugely beneficial to her, the bad news was that her nose was far too small for her to hang on to any money. 'Easy come, easy go,' he told her, smiling.

Well, that was two hundred dollars gone already, Ryan decided, whistling softly under his breath. Chloe apparently thought so too, as she started pushing back her chair and getting up to leave. 'Wait!' said the fortune teller making her sit down again. 'Something important you must know.'

'Great!' Ryan said aloud and immediately wished he hadn't as two pairs of eyes turned on him accusingly. 'I'll, erm, see you outside then,' he told Chloe. He didn't need a fortune teller to tell him his time was up.

Ryan wandered under a decorative stone arch and into the lush green calm of the Good Wish Garden which, he hoped, would cool his burning curiosity. He perched on the low wall beside an ornamental pond where a notice expressly forbade the release of terra-pin. No one seemed to have told the terrapins though as there were plenty there already. Three of them skimmed the surface, blinking at a woman who had crouched down to coo over them.

After what seemed like an age, Chloe came padding towards him, the thin slip polka dot dress she was wearing making her look effortlessly cool, elegant and hopelessly unavailable. The tug of desire he always felt at every first sight of her was momentarily subdued by a sense of hopelessness. He wished he could give her the secure future she craved, but when he thought about what had happened to his parents he was too afraid that was one thing he couldn't guarantee. Chloe had wasted too much looking after her father; now she deserved someone who would take care of her.

As she drew closer he could see that her face, in contrast to her body language, was a picture of confusion. He sat straighter noticing her frown as she stared blankly around her. When she finally saw him and registered where he was sitting, her eyes widened.

'What's up? You look as if you've seen a ghost,' he said, patting the space beside him rather more casually than he felt. If he found out the fortune teller had taken advantage of his departure to employ scare tactics, he was in for a big, bearded and rude surprise.

Chloe blew out so slowly that a small splash in the water beside them made them both jump. A baby terrapin had popped up to the surface and floated up close by.

'The four-legged creature!' he thought he heard Chloe mutter before lifting her puzzled gaze to his.

'What? It's a terrapin, a very small one, I grant you,' he lifted his camera too late as the tiny reptile disappeared into the water's shadowy green depths. 'So what did the guy have to tell you that was so important?

Chloe shot him another strange look. 'Well, I honestly thought it was all nonsense, but then he pinched a fold of skin on my palm and told me I'd had a 'little contact lens' problem. The spooky thing is, that only a couple of weeks ago, I had a really nasty bout of conjunctivitis and I really thought I'd be doomed to wear my horrible specs for this trip until it cleared up at the last minute.'

'And?' He knew how short-sighted Chloe was and how much she hated her thick glasses, but why was she so shaken? He patted her hand. 'It was a lucky guess, that's all. He spotted your lenses and calculated that you might have been affected by the climate or the flight. Good observational skills, nothing freaky.'

Chloe chewed her lip then took a deep breath. 'Yes,' she agreed, 'how else would they do it?'

'So,' he said, enjoying the warmth of her bare arm next to his, 'what was that about the four-legged creature?'

'That' said Chloe, darting a quick, suspicious look at the ornamental pool, 'was what's commonly known as a load of baloney.' She straightened up, smoothed out her dress and looked into his face. 'And now it's my turn to make a suggestion. Are you free this evening, because there's something I'd really like to do.'

He had a feeling she was using a diversionary tactic to throw him off the scent, but Ryan no longer cared. A wave of satisfaction washed over him; he was going on a date with Chloe.

★   ★   ★

A full moon hung low in the sky above Victoria Harbour that night, dwarfing the glittering towers and skyscrapers that rose on either side and spilling a wash of silver across ripples of inky blue water. Chloe stood to breathe in the sight and keep it in her mind's eye for when she was back home. Taking the Star Ferry across the harbour from the Kowloon Peninsula to Hong Kong Island and back again, was, she'd decided early in the week, absolutely her favourite thing to do in Hong Kong.

When Ryan challenged her to write the feature text in exchange for his photos, she'd treated herself to a pretty notebook with a gorgeous turquoise silk cover. Her notes, which had been stilted and self-conscious at first, developed from the moment she'd first set foot on the ferry.

Her writing voice grew stronger and more confident as she described something that was so much more than cheap transport for local workers. Like so many tourists before her, she'd fallen in love with the romance of the vessels with their star-related names and nostalgic green and white livery, the old-fashioned sailor suits worn by the staff and the star patterns punched in the wooden seats. All the magic of casting off and embarking on a short voyage that charmed her with its sights and sounds every time. Looking back at her notes, she could see Ryan was right; there was nothing like personal experience to bring flat words to life. Rather than writing to order for Guy, which was her customary style, she was using her own words and expressions and telling her own story.

'When it comes to enjoying the night lights of Hong Kong, this beats the laser show they put on for the tourists hands down,' Ryan said, smiling at her. 'We'll get a much better view from the boat.'

Yes, there was that, she thought to herself and it would make her research so much more authentic if she had a good-looking man beside her rather than sitting there all on her own like Lucy Loser. Despite the warm charge she felt at Ryan's touch as he gently guided her through the passengers waiting to board, Chloe knew on good authority that her heart was perfectly safe.

'I see two men in your life,' the fortune teller had solemnly prophesied, 'one dark, one fair. One man is your future, the other is your past.'

'I asked about my career not my love

life!' Chloe had insisted. 'I don't need to know how many children I'm having.'

'Two,' the fortune teller told her, giving her a twinkly smile above his gold-rimmed glasses.

Chloe sighed and rolled her eyes. 'Well now you've told me that, you'd better let me know if either of these men is a likely candidate to be the father.'

It was the fortune teller's turn to sigh. He bent over her palm again, and studied it carefully before withdrawing in a paroxysm of laughter.

'Well, share the joke, then,' Chloe said, trying not be offended that she was the cause of so much amusement.

'You shall know by dark waters and the four-legged creature whether the fair man is fair or the dark-haired man is — '

'Don't tell me, let me guess — '

'End of consultation,' the fortune teller announced abruptly. 'You go now.'

Pah! What a load of nonsense, Chloe thought to herself again as she and Ryan boarded the ferry. The only

four-legged creatures she'd come anywhere close to that evening were
melting mouthfuls of barbecued pork
tucked inside miniature glazed buns
which she'd enjoyed in a fabulous dim
sum restaurant Ryan had recom-
mended. She was a bit sorry she hadn't
let him take her there sooner because
then they could have fitted in a couple
of visits. The succession of steamer
baskets brought to their table were
veritable boxes of delight opening to
reveal many exquisite morsels, like the
fluffiest shrimp and crab dumplings.
However she was full, content and
ready to enjoy the rest of the evening
with her good friend Ryan safe in the
knowledge that although there was a lot
of dark water, there wasn't a four-
legged creature in sight.

A night breeze blew through the open
sides of the boat, just cool enough to
raise the goose-bumps on her bare arm.
Nothing to do with Ryan, of course,
because there were no signs to suggest
that anything momentous was about to

happen. It wasn't tempting fate at all to enjoy the frisson of pleasure when Ryan draped his arm round her shoulders. She leaned in, feeling the reassuring warmth of his body, breathing in the sandalwood and cedar scent of him, blissfully ignoring the little voice inside chattering, *right here, right now, don't think about what tomorrow might bring.* Where else could she dream if not in this moonlit in-between world of indigo shadows and hidden depths?

When she was little, her mum used to sing a song to her about catching moonbeams in a jar, but, tonight, gliding across a silver path on a purple sea was good enough. Instead of yearning for something that was forever out of reach, she would content herself with the moment. So she sat back, reached for Ryan's hand, wrapped herself closer in his embrace and soaked up the atmosphere of a unique city that looked both ways, to the ancient and modern. A skyline where light displays lit the glass and steel facades of glittering commercial buildings and colourful laser beams criss-crossed the crow-black sky beneath the moon.

She smiled to herself as Ryan dropped a kiss on her hair and if a small part of herself was willing time to slow down so she could hang on to the moment, that was fine too. Yet every turn of the ship's engine took them nearer to the shore and closer to reality.

Her attention was captured by a display on one of the soaring buildings before them, where swirling white lights danced and dazzled. Utterly spellbound by the clever technology that created such intricate patterns, Chloe watched as waves of lights resolved themselves into swaying branches, falling leaves and — surely not? — a leaping deer. Finally, as if written just for her to really slam the message home, the swirling lights came together and fell away once more until she found herself staring at a series of letters which spelled out a word. *Hope.*

'Oh my god,' she said, breathing out slowly. 'It's you, Ryan.'

His hand came up and he traced the outline of her cheek with warm fingers. 'Of course it is.' She could hear the smile in his voice. 'I've been here all the time. Didn't you know?'

She swallowed and lifted her face, trying to read his expression in the dark. He slipped his fingers through her hair and breathed her name, shockingly intimate, achingly familiar. Seconds passed like minutes as he cupped her head in his hand and drew her towards him. And then the night exploded into colour and heat as his mouth came down on hers, at first sweet and gentle, then urgently as she responded with joy and wonder and in the certainty that it was meant to be.

6

Ryan leaned closer to Chloe so that she could see the monitor of his camera more clearly. 'Look, you're floating on air.' The quiet composition pleased him; her pale feet, in the bottom third of the frame, were set against the teal blue of Tung Chung Bay which sparkled beneath the glass floor of their cable cabin as they soared towards the lush greenery of Lantau Island. He might almost have captured a sylph in flight. One, he thought smiling to himself, who wore red nail polish.

Except he was only too aware that it wasn't some elusive mythical spirit of the air so tantalisingly within his reach, but a warm, living woman, the one he'd gathered into him after the passion was temporarily spent, the curve of her bottom cupped into his lap, their breathing in harmony. Coupled together until the heat of the morning sun through the pale blinds had eased them apart.

As she bent her head to examine the image he closed his eyes, momentarily assailed by a sensuous haze of perfume and warm skin, a potent scent memory of the night before. He raised his hand, lifted her glossy dark hair and let it fall through his fingers hardly daring to believe his luck.

They were fortunate to have been granted a gin-clear view for the breath-taking sky trail; there would be no second chances, not on this trip anyway. Tomorrow, they'd be boarding a plane and heading for home. He only wished someone could tell him what would happen when they landed. He'd managed to puzzle out that another night with Chloe hadn't been enough yet they had both had real lives to return to, careers waiting for them and very different ideas of what they wanted for themselves.

Beside him, Chloe laughed and braced herself as the cables swept their apparently flimsy gondola into a station to turn. He smiled at her, enjoying her excitement.

'I hope you won't feel disappointed when we get there,' he warned, just in case. 'The journey's the most spectacular part of this attraction.'

'What's not to love about a Big Buddha?' Chloe said, wrinkling her nose at him. 'The largest seated bronze Buddha in the world. How could I come all this way and not see it when I might not get another chance?'

He lifted her hand to his lips and kissed it thinking about last chances. He wasn't that much of a spiritual person, nevertheless he could do with a little enlightenment about what the future held. An unsettling sensation of the ground rushing towards him, as they glided up the green slopes of the Lantau Country Park ahead, instinctively made him hold on to Chloe more tightly. He wasn't normally the slightest bit bothered by heights, so he had a strong suspicion that his sudden disorientation was more to do with his heart than his head.

At the summit in Ngong Ping Village, they ate noodles and spicy fried fish balls. He snapped Chloe pulling a face at her first bite before giving it a thumbs up and digging in. Colourful stalls selling fans in rainbow hues, coolie hats, slippers and trinkets provided plenty of ways to part souvenir hunters from their cash, but Chloe was content to just browse the displays.

'Two hundred and sixty-eight steps, right?'

'I'll take your word for it,' Ryan agreed, knowing she was right; general knowledge wasn't something anyone could revise, but Chloe's research background and sharp memory meant she often came up with the most surprising facts.

'Last one to the top, buys dinner tonight.' She grinned, nodding towards the steep flight of steps where a constant stream of people climbed to see the massive seated bronze statue of Buddha.

'I'm not sure I feel especially enlightened,' she admitted at the top, 'just hot after climbing all those steps, though both the statue and the views from the top *are* spectacular. I just wish . . . '

Suddenly her mood changed, the sadness creeping in from nowhere.

'What do you wish?' He quickly guided her to one side of the giant statues rising above them, where the views were of jagged peaks rising from thickly-wooded slopes. The breeze blew her hair back from her face revealing her troubled dark eyes.

'Oh, I don't know, I guess it's just the thought of going home again, back to real life. Also, I know it's daft, but I just thought how nice it would be if I could tell my mum about this trip. I some-times forget she's not here any more.'

The catch in her voice tugged at his heart. He gave her shoulder what he hoped was a comforting squeeze. 'So tell her, Chloe. Just say the words out loud and let them go. I'm sure if your mum could see you right now, she'd be happy for you.'

She fiddled with her sunglasses and gave him an awkward smile. 'My mum didn't really do happy. She never ever felt she was good enough at what she did. Always judged herself too harshly.'

'That's a bit of a lesson, isn't it?' He couldn't stop himself saying. 'You're too hard on yourself at times, it's been good to see you relax and unwind this week. But you said yourself that your mother had been unwell for a long time and that takes its toll on everyone. Illness, pain, frustration — all those things can change people's personalities, drag them down.' He thought of his own father.

'Yes,' she said in a low voice. 'Yes, Mum was ill; she suffered quite badly from depression. She was one of Dad's students, so he was quite a bit older than her. Although they loved each other, they had unrealistic expectations of what they wanted from each other.'

'In what way?' he asked, stroking her shoulder.

'Well, Mum expected Dad to be

endlessly wise and clever and he wanted her to stay as she was, to be the adoring young wife he'd brought home from honeymoon. When I came along, I feel like maybe it added to the strain on their relationship. I think Dad slightly resented her attention being divided and didn't give her the help she needed and Mum hinted she hadn't been able to reach her potential because she'd stayed at home to look after me.'

'But that wasn't your fault, Chloe. That was something they should have discussed and sorted out between themselves. You were only a child.'

'That's true,' she agreed, 'but that's why, when I was little, I wanted to be a doctor when I grew up, a real doctor not an academic like Dad. I thought I could fix the part of Mum that was broken and make them both happy again or prescribe some pills that would give her back her smile. Of course, in the end, it was a bottle of pills that gave her peace, though not the kind Dad and I wished for her.'

'Oh, Chloe,' he pulled her to him and hugged her tightly. 'Why didn't you tell me sooner?'

She heaved a sigh into his chest then pulled away and looked up at him. 'Honestly? Because I didn't want to frighten you off. I mean, my mother's mental health isn't exactly the stuff of small talk, is it?' The sunglasses went back on. Brave red lipstick making her smile almost convincing. 'Besides, we're here for a good time, not for an intense, emotional time. Isn't that your philosophy?'

He felt stung. 'No, because I'm not shallow.' He drew a deep breath. 'I believe that every day is a gift and every minute is precious, and let me tell you, Chloe, these moments with you have been very precious indeed. We owe it to ourselves to make the most of today because none of us knows what tomorrow will bring.'

'The thing is,' she said, stepping back. 'I *can* see into the future and I know in two weeks' time when Dad remarries and I have to accept that Mum really won't be coming back that I'll be facing the situation on my own.'

He spread his hands in a gesture of helplessness. 'Chloe, we've talked about this. I've got work commitments.'

'Can't you take a weekend off?' she pleaded.

'I'm sorry,' he said, very gently, 'but this is important to me. I've been thinking about this project for a long time and I can't just abandon it now. But that doesn't mean that I don't want to carry on seeing you.'

'I'm sorry too,' she replied quietly. 'I don't know what I was thinking of ruining the moment by going over old ground. You'd think that standing under the world's biggest Buddha would stop all those negative thoughts! Buddhism's supposed to free you from the past, isn't it? I shouldn't have said anything and it's not fair to you.'

'Not fair? Chloe, we spent last night together. It feels as if you're saying it's okay to share your body with me, but not your thoughts.'

She shrugged, the sunglasses still masking her eyes. 'Last night was probably a mistake too. I lived in the moment for once in my life, but I don't want to live with uncertainty in the future, Ryan. I want a partner who'll be there for me when I need support. I want to know where I stand.'

A couple walked up beside them, turning to pose for a selfie against the dramatic scenery, laughing as they took their shots before exchanging smug kisses. Chloe took advantage of the interruption to try to slip away, but she wasn't escaping that easily.

'You didn't give any indication there was anything wrong last night,' he said, grabbing her arm. 'Far from it. You were with me every step of the way. Every breath.'

The couple, still within earshot, swapped mock-horrified glances and scarpered, giggling.

'It was you,' she said, her voice thick with emotion, 'who said you were a 'just for now man'. And I should have listened. Last night was magical, as it always is with you, Ryan. But magic doesn't last, does it? It's just an illusion; my mistake was make-believing it could be anything else.' The sunglasses came off again and her sad smile tore at his heart. 'I've had a wonderful time with you, Ryan, but it's never going to work out between us, is it? We have very different expectations of what we want from life. You're carefree and I'm careful . . . we'd only get frustrated and end up hurting each other.'

She stood up on tiptoe and kissed his cheek. 'I'm going back to the hotel now. I'll see you at the airport tomorrow, naturally, and then we've only got to get through the flight.'

'Hang on,' he said, catching her elbow as she started to walk away. 'Don't I get a say in this?'

She shook her head, looked at his hand on her arm and sighed. 'Sorry, Ryan but this isn't about you or me — it's about doing what's best for us.'

And as she replaced the sunglasses with a gesture of finality, he thought he saw the glitter of tears. She walked towards the steps, a slight figure in cream linen trousers and navy striped T-shirt. Could he really stand there and watch her go when she needed comfort and reassurance? But what did he have to say that she wanted to hear?

He ran a hand through his hair in frustration. Magic, she'd said, but he was the one left feeling as if he'd been sliced in two. If she didn't believe he had more to offer her than a box of tricks, there was no point in running after her. Paralysed with uncertainty, conflicting emotions warring within him, he watched as Chloe reached the steps and began her descent. She didn't look back, but he kept his eyes on her anyway, watching until the striped T-shirt blurred and was lost in a rainbow of clothing colours. It was too late.

7

Over the next two weeks, October gave way to November in a blaze of flame-coloured leaves. As Chloe walked towards the modern apartment block it looked as if the morning sunshine had burnished the trees with gold, yet something about all that bright beauty set against the blue sky only made her feel sad. Instead of being excited that she was about to view a flat that could be hers for the taking she ached for everything she missed.

Perhaps it was just as well that the nights were getting longer. The topsy-turvy working hours she was trying to adjust to might not seem so arduous when the sliver of daylight was dovetailed by extended darkness at either end. And when the winter really set in, she would be properly settled in her new job and too busy to notice the weather. Unlike Ryan who was presumably watching every slant of the light as it hit the side of a mountain somewhere in the middle of nowhere.

Somehow, she managed to raise a smile at Guy on the other side of the building's glass entrance doors, as he made a show of dangling a set of keys at her before buzzing her in. Whereas Ryan tended to dress from a stormy palette of greys and black and most of his clothes seemed to have done months of outdoor service, Guy, as always, was impeccably presented. He pressed cool lips to her cheek in greeting and Chloe numbly followed him across the polished stone floor of the lobby.

I must stop wondering where Ryan is, or who he's with or what he's doing, she reminded herself, coming to at the sight of her own reflection staring glumly back at her as the mirrored lift climbed upwards. They'd said their painful and awkward goodbyes at the airport, a tacit acceptance on both sides that their lives were running in different directions. For all Ryan had said about approaching travel magazines with a ready-made feature about Hong Kong, he hadn't yet sent her the ten photographs he'd promised. Not that Guy had shown any interest when she'd suggested a travel feature for the programme to him either. Still, today was about deciding on her future home, rather than living in the past. Then she noticed Guy running an appraising gaze over her and felt even more depressed.

'You've lost weight,' he said. 'It suits you. Carb cutting, right? It was about time you realised all those biscuits you love to guzzle with your tea weren't doing you any favours. Hey, if you play your cards right, I might even consider taking you out this evening. It's about time we celebrated our renewed partnership. And don't worry,' he added before she could reply, 'I can always give you time to change out of those old things first.'

Chloe took a deep breath. The Heartbreak Diet might have helped her shed a few pounds but nothing would ever deflate Guy's overblown ego. Wilma, in her arms, stuck her head out of Chloe's open coat where Guy had demanded she be hidden and loyally took offence on her behalf, yapping her disapproval.

'Look at her, daft animal,' Guy observed, bright with forced affection, 'thinks she's seen another dog in the mirror. Tone it down, sweetheart,' he said, leaning forward and tickling the suspicious dachshund rather warily, 'this is a nice, quiet place; you don't want to give people the wrong impression.'

Wilma curled her upper lip and snarled.

'Elvis,' said Guy, clicking his fingers and pointing at her. 'Very good, Wilma.' Just then the lift stopped and the doors opened. 'This way, ladies,' he went on, 'you're going to love this.'

Chloe, still carrying Wilma, followed him to a bland front door in a faux dark wood pattern that owed nothing to a tree and hoped he was right. A smooth exterior didn't necessarily equate with a complete lack of charm, she reminded herself. Despite his utterly patronising manner, even Guy, Mr Superficial himself, had proved he could be thoughtful. He *had* gone out of his way, after all, *and* chased up favours to help her find somewhere to live because he knew that struggling into work from Kent was half killing her. That had to count for something.

Beneath the dark overcoat he was wearing, Guy was dressed in his off-duty mode of slim-fitting caramel cords and a sky-blue cashmere jumper. His thick, dark blonde hair was slicked back from his face but was sufficiently tousled to suggest that all it would take was a sweep of fingers for it to fall into place, his pale blue eyes gleamed with self-satisfaction and when he grinned back at her, his teeth . . .

'Guy!' She giggled into Wilma's soft, chestnut head. 'You've gone and bought yourself a Hollywood smile!'

'And?' He scowled. Or would have,

Chloe guessed, if the botox she suspected he'd had done on his frown lines, allowed. 'I'm only doing what everyone else in the business is doing,' he pointed out. 'Just being a serious professional and taking care of my appearance for my public. People have expectations of how celebrities should look these days. You should think about that too, if you want to get on.'

'But, Guy, you're a radio presenter! Not, of course, that it means you don't have to bother,' she added quickly, seeing a flicker of hurt, insecurity perhaps, behind that diffident expression. 'Your teeth look great. Much better than they were. I'm not saying you had teeth like railings, but . . . '

'Chloe, sweetheart,' he said, sounding weary. 'Shall we concentrate on what the flat looks like instead? And try to bear in mind how lucky you are to get a foot through the door. These apartments don't come up very often. You're effectively getting the chance to try before you buy — renting privately and, may I point out, very reasonably, while my contact in the States is making up her mind about where her bread's buttered. It's a dead cert that she'll stay over there and put this place on the market, at which point you'll be able to save her a whole heap of estate agent fees. And — ' he added, nodding his head pointedly at Wilma, ' — what the eye doesn't see the heart won't grieve about. Win, win. Now, do you want to see inside or not?'

He was right; few rented flats permitted pets and that started to sway her opinion. Maybe it was because Guy had actually done something nice for Wilma or perhaps it was because she suddenly remembered how self-conscious he was about anything that might be regarded as a personal flaw and the strenuous effort he made to keep up appearances, that a remnant of the old affection bubbled up for him.

Somewhere very close to the surface was the boy from a deprived background, the one whose mum could never afford to buy him the things other children had, who grew up to be the successful man working hard to put as much distance as possible between the present and his humble beginnings. Even if that did mean he could be very intolerant about dog hairs.

'Of course, I want to see inside,' she said, giving him a proper smile. 'And thank you. You've been great. You know I can't possibly stay at Dad's once Emma moves in. It's hard enough having the woman in the house but I can certainly do without watching Dad dancing attendance on her.'

'All yours,' he said, handing her the key. '"The woman' as you put it, is your father's intended so he's allowed to dance attendance on her. And frankly, it's about time you left home. You should have done it years ago.'

Trust Guy to spoil the moment. 'That's not fair. Dad needed me to look after him,' she replied, irritation and Wilma fidgeting making her fumble the lock at her initial attempt.

'Hmm. I got the impression that your father's always been rather good at looking after himself. So long as he had his books, he was happy.'

It was true that her dad hadn't been there for her as much as she would have liked after her mother's death; they'd both been devastated, but Chloe had managed to rally more quickly because she was so anxious about her father. He'd always been forgetful about eating, especially when he was engrossed in his studies, but after her mother's death he immersed himself in his work and became so careless about his health that he'd lost an alarming amount of weight. Chloe still remembered the small triumph represented by every meal she persuaded him to eat.

'Mind you,' Guy observed over her shoulder. 'Life in the ivory tower couldn't have been all about work, could it? Your dad still managed to find himself a fiancée. And, yes, I know it's put your nose out of joint a bit, but it's also given you the kick up the backside you needed to finally fly the nest. I mean what have you done with your life?'

'I was saving money,' Chloe said, stung even though she was struggling to keep hold of Wilma, who was desperate to get down. 'It takes a long time to find the deposit for a mortgage on my salary.'

'Patience, sweetheart, you're earning more than you were when we were out in the sticks, remember. Let's see what we can do at the end of your probationary period. Besides, a mortgage clearly wasn't the first thing on your mind when you blew all that money on an expensive holiday. Be honest, a cosy arrangement living under Daddy's roof suited you until another woman came along, didn't it? Well, hallelujah, it was high time you moved on.'

Hot and cross, Chloe finally managed to open the door. Guy, one hand in the small of her back, ushered her in. 'Congratulations,' he said silkily. 'Stop sulking, you're a grown-up at last. Welcome to the rest of your life.'

She opened her mouth to tell him that, actually, losing her mum in such dreadful circumstances had made her grow up pretty fast, but deep inside another voice was whispering that maybe he was right. Her dad, undemonstrative as he was, had at least been a reassuring presence in her life. He was a man of few words, but his grateful smile when she made him a hot drink and placed it silently on his desk, showed his appreciation. It was enough for her to know that he was always there: she was loved, she was safe, she had continuity. That was the danger of falling for someone like Ryan; even when he was physically there, he was forever out of reach, his emotions frozen behind a square of glass. No wonder she'd clung to security. Outside, in the big wide world, your heart could be stolen away and broken.

One thing that could be said for Guy was that you knew exactly where you stood with him. He made no secret of his ambitions; he was career-driven, focused and determined not just to work his way to the top of the tree, but also to surround himself with all the material possessions such as the expensive car, the luxury flat and the designer gear which reflected that success. In a way she had to admire him, not that she was impressed by rich men or shows of wealth, but you couldn't fault his commitment, or his work ethic.

He wasn't, for all his mild threat of taking her out later that evening, even that much of a party animal. What he liked most of all, she learned during their relationship, was to lounge in front of the latest TV box set with a ready meal — nothing too exotic — and a good glass of wine. Although he had been a bit fussy about food or drink splatters on his white sofas. A rock and roll lifestyle, it wasn't, but there was a lot to be said for a man who was such a home bird.

Wilma sprung for freedom, skittering off along the freshly-painted hall, her claws tap-tapping on the laminate floor.

Chloe, blinking as the low sunshine through the long glass windows bounced off the white walls, followed her on the brief tour of what was essentially one large living room with a small kitchen area at one end, a double bedroom and a luxury bathroom. It was compact, it was ultra-modern and there wasn't an iota of character, but neither did it have draughty windows which let in the distant hiss of the sea breaking on the shore and a large bearded man playing with her feelings. Heck, she'd make herself love it.

'It's perfect,' she declared. 'Thank you.'

'Admit it,' said Guy, nudging her as he stood beside her, 'I did a good job finding this place, didn't I?'

'What do you want?' she sighed. 'A medal?'

'Another chance?' he said quietly.

Chloe was about to protest when he caught hold of her hands and turned her, gently, to face him.

'I behaved like a total arse before, trying to make you choose between me and Wilma. I should have known it was the quickest way to drive you away. It was only because I'd got my place just as I liked it, with all the cream carpets and sofas, that I couldn't stand the thought of muddy paws everywhere. Or sitting on a half-eaten dog chew. After you broke things off, I realised that none of the possessions meant anything without someone to appreciate them with me. It was a tough lesson.'

'Well, that's good,' she said and looked up to catch his unmasked expression, the hopelessness in his eyes which flooded her with compassion. Chloe's head swam. There was no doubting Guy's sincerity and hadn't he proved it too, offering her a wonderful career opportunity and finding her a place to live? But starting again? She couldn't do that, could she?

He leaned forward and rested his head gently against hers so that she could smell the fresh green scent of his expensive aftershave, feel the familiarity of his lean body. 'Think about it, Chloe.

We make a good team. Haven't we proved that as colleagues? I don't want to rush you into anything. Move in here and get used to your own space, get used to the job and a new city. But let's find some time for us too.'

Chloe fumbled for something tactful to say. The wrong phrase and she could find herself out of a job pretty quickly and then she would have no alternative but to stay at home playing gooseberry to her dad and his new bride.

'You don't have to say anything yet,' Guy said with a rueful smile. 'Just give it some thought. I know it's early days for you but having you in my life would give meaning to all my hard work. I wouldn't be lonely any more. I'd have someone to come home to.'

A bit like her with Wilma, Chloe thought in passing before her gaze travelled to his lips. A dependable companion. Not like Ryan. There was a lot to be said for security. Guy bent his head and Chloe froze as she realised he really was about to kiss her. Stepping away could be critical to her career, but on the other hand, one kiss for old time's sake might help her to decide whether or not there was any chance they could start again as a couple. Guy had admitted he'd been in the wrong, wasn't that a start? She closed her eyes and braced herself, trying to shut out all thoughts of Ryan. As she waited, she was dimly aware in the background of the sound of Wilma tripping towards them.

'Jesus!' Guy backed off before impact, gasping and spluttering for breath.

'Wilma!' Chloe choked out, swatting at the air, trying to bat the ghastly smell away. 'Did you have to? I'm *so* sorry, Guy.'

'No problem,' he said bravely, 'I guess I'll have to earn her trust as well as yours.'

Chloe shot a look at Wilma who trotted off with the satisfied swagger of someone who knows their work is done. Wilma had adored Ryan and his rude basset, Fred. But she was not about to let a flatulent dachshund rule her love life. 'Guy,' she asked, 'would you like to come to Dad and Emma's wedding with me?'

8

Winter waves crashed on the beach a few streets away as Ryan stood outside a small Victorian terraced cottage the other side of Little Spitmarsh from his own sprawling villa, waiting for his cousin to answer. It was early and seagulls soared overhead, their mournful cries lamenting the empty seafront and absence of tourists nursing greasy packets of chips. Fred looked up at him with trusting eyes making Ryan feel worse than he already did which was quite a surprise given how bad he felt.

'Running away again?' Tansy remarked, as she opened the door.

'Tansy, I have a job to do, remember?' Ryan shouted over Fred's enthusiastic howling as she stepped back in her hallway to let them in. 'If you're sore about being lumbered with Fred, just tell me. You're an angel to take care of him so often, but I can always make alternative arrangements in future.'

'In case you hadn't noticed, Little Spitmarsh isn't exactly teeming with kennels.' With a shake of her bright marigold curls, made fiercer by the mustard jumper she was wearing over a red tartan mini skirt and thick green tights, Tansy turned away. Flounced, you could say, thought Ryan, except Fred rather spoiled her stage exit, expressing his delight at seeing her again by enthusiastically launching himself as close as he could reach to her bottom, almost lifting her off her feet.

'Especially,' she spluttered, regaining her balance, 'kennels willing to accept bassets with such bad manners. You'd never catch Vic or Bob behaving so disgracefully.'

'Oh no, they're too busy trying to slaughter every bird that dares venture into your garden. The Siamese cat Kray twins. No wonder the Cats Protection people were so pleased to get rid of them. Anyway, you've neglected to say hello to either of us,' Ryan said, swooping to kiss her on the cheek. 'He was just reminding you he was there. What's wrong? Things all right between you and Duncan?'

As she knelt to make a fuss of Fred, she waved her left hand to show him the engagement ring was back in place, the solitaire diamond twinkling at him. So it wasn't that bugging her then, although her on-off relationship with her childhood sweetheart baffled him. Talk about couldn't live together, couldn't live apart. But who was he to criticise when the most enduring partnership in his life was the one he shared with his dog?

'What makes you think there's a problem between me and Duncan?' Tansy asked, straightening up.

'Because the poor guy's been doomed ever since you hit him with a spade for daring to propose to you,' Ryan pointed out, not unreasonably, he felt.

'Once! I hit him with a spade once! A plastic spade at that. It was my sixth birthday and with a five month age gap between us he was too immature for me then. Anyway, apart from the cut to his eyebrow, most of the damage was to his pride.'

'I'm surprised he ever came back for more,' he added, following her as she led the way into her tiny sitting room. 'Three proposals and you two still aren't married. I reckon there's something in the family genes that tells us we won't do well in captivity and triggers the self-preservation response.'

'Nope, that doesn't wash. Your mum and dad were one of the happiest couples I've ever known, I always loved going to your house because of them. Even now, they're not doing so badly.'

Ryan left that observation where it was. It still pained him to think how changed his father was, how much his mother had given up, how restricted their lifestyle had become as a result of what had happened.

There was a tiny pause before Tansy continued speaking. 'Duncan and I may have, um, a volatile relationship but we'll be fine.' She flopped onto the purple velvet sofa and patted the space next to her. Ryan threw a couple of cushions out the way to make the space bigger but no sooner had he sat down when Fred clambered up and sprawled out between them.

Tansy narrowed her eyes at him. 'Self-preservation or cowardice? How long are you going to keep trying to escape your feelings for Chloe?'

'What now?' Ryan did his best to laugh. 'There's nothing to escape as you put it. Chloe broke it off because she didn't think we had enough in common. She wants a guaranteed future and I want — '

'To disappear up a mountain in the middle of winter. It *was* this weekend you were supposed to be going to a wedding, wasn't it?'

'The weather will be perfect for what I'm trying to achieve.' Ryan folded his arms. 'And, as it turns out, if I *had* agreed to go the wedding, I would have had to let Chloe down at the last moment. In the end it was her decision, Tans, she was the one who wanted us to go our separate ways.'

'Uh-huh. So you chose the weather over the woman. Look how well that worked out for you. You could have been quaffing champagne with the woman of your dreams in a lovely room in some nice little boutique hotel in picturesque Canterbury.'

Next time his heart was bleeding, he made a mental note, he wouldn't blab to Tansy who had a memory like an elephant and was worse than Fred with a bone about letting go.

'Snowdonia is more than pictur-esque, it's breath-taking — especially in winter — that's why I'm going, to capture the sight of those gleaming peaks against the pale blue sky.'

Thinking about gleaming peaks and drinking champagne wasn't doing him any good, it only conjured up images of a sharing a huge bubble bath, him at one end, Chloe up the other, foam sliding all over her wet curves.

'It's a bit short on king-sized beds and crisp cotton bedlinen, though,' Tansy chimed in. 'Plus, you won't get laid after all the hard work.'

Ryan reached for a cushion and stuffed it — in a cousinly sort of way — in her face. With a great effort he dragged his mind away from the carnally uplifting to the aesthetically pleasing and life-affirming. 'I couldn't turn this commission down. It's easy money; it's no sacrifice to be in the mountains and the photographs almost take themselves. At this time of year, the low light makes those craggy contours look positively majestic, the waterfalls are swollen and heavy from the autumn rain and deep blue pools suddenly appear through the swirling cloud. It's inspirational.'

'Fair point, Dylan Thomas.' Tansy nodded. 'I suppose you're also going to tell me that you can only feel the magic of these wilderness places when you're alone.'

Between them, Fred snored loudly.

Ryan sighed. 'I'm sorry about dumping Fred on you, but those legs of his aren't really built for scree slopes.'

'Fred is not the one I'm worried about,' said Tansy holding up her hand. 'And don't tell me about scree slopes. You're supposed to be taking pretty pictures not re-enacting *Touching the Void*. I thought you'd be safe once you'd finished with all those hard news features abroad.'

He frowned at her. 'Of course, I'll be safe — I've hostile environment training, remember?'

'Now I'm worried about you falling off a mountain . . . ' she broke off with a small moan. 'Ryan, you haven't been yourself since you came back from Hong Kong, you're not planning on doing something stupid, are you?'

He shook his head in disbelief. 'I'm not about to throw myself off the highest ridge, if that's what you're thinking. I'm a happy man. I'm my own boss, my job takes me to the most amazing places, I'm free to do pretty much as I please — and,' he patted Fred, 'I have a faithful companion waiting for me at home.'

One who accepted him as he was, never complained about his comings and goings and took every day as it came. None of which had been enough for Chloe who was probably throwing her suitcase in the back of Guy Bradshaw's Mercedes about now.

Tansy looked at him sadly. 'I hope your freedom — ' she made little quotation marks with her fingers, ' — is worth the price of being cold and lonely. I still think you're going to look back and realise that you let the woman you loved slide through your hands.'

'Love?' he laughed. 'What happened to getting laid? It was a fling, Tansy. She was rebounding like one of Fred's rubber balls and she just happened to collide with me.'

'And you're protesting too much,' said Tansy, leaning forwards. 'I'm worried about you, Ryan. You can't keep running away from your feelings forever. Think about that when you're alone in the mountains. And when you get back, give Chloe a call.'

For what reason? Weddings bred weddings and the last thing he needed to hear was that she was engaged to Guy.

'Just concentrate on finding your own happy ever after, will you?' he said, getting up. Well, one of them had to get lucky.

* * *

On the opposite side of the country, the following afternoon, in a grand old building which sat well in its grounds, but had apparently suffered a 'foot-ballers' wives meets country house pastiche' during its transformation into a hotel, Chloe was seated at the front of one of the most hideous function rooms she'd ever encountered. How much say, she wondered, shuddering at the calamine lotion pink walls and huge pink organza bows hugging shiny white covered chairs, had her father had in the choice of venue? What her mother would have made of it beggared belief, but at least Chloe was certain she would have approved of the understated outfit she'd chosen with, admittedly, fairly perfunctory effort. A finely pleated pearl grey skirt which accentuated her neat waist, a little beaded silvery top which was dressy without being showy and a navy cover-up with matching high-heeled courts.

'Very sophisticated,' had been Guy's comment, 'if a little sombre.' Chloe nodded. She was there to please her dad; all she wanted to do was get through the day. Sombre was how she felt and her outfit struck just the right note for the occasion; elegant, appropriate but not over the top. Which was more than could be said for the mother of the bride, whose comfortable frame was draped in exuberant raspberry and silver devoré with a fascinator to match. Her anxious expression suggested that she might, perhaps, be slightly regretting such a bold choice.

Or had Emma put her up to it?

'Look at all this,' Chloe muttered under her breath to Guy, who, as usual, was faultlessly turned out, although looked rather as if he was auditioning for a role as Bond. 'Why on earth would they want all this palaver at their age? They're not exactly love's young dreams are they?'

'Come on,' said Guy, 'they're allowed to celebrate, aren't they? Didn't you say this was Emma's first time? A girl's allowed to be a bit of a princess on the happiest day of her life.'

Hardly a girl, thought Chloe, as the first notes of '(Everything I Do) I Do It For You' momentarily distracted her. Sheesh! Where had that come from? Not her dad's music collection, certainly. Everyone rose as Bryan Adams implored them to search their hearts. Any minute now they'd all see what the blushing bride was wearing, Chloe only hoped her dad wasn't about to come face-to-face with a large meringue. She flicked a gaze to him to see how he was faring and was stunned when he looked over his shoulder, caught her eye and gave her a wide smile. Years had dropped from him; he looked nervous but excited and happier than she'd ever seen him. Her throat tightened and suddenly she had to swallow hard as it struck her that this ceremony, which she thought was all about placating Emma, was equally important and meaningful to him.

She glanced to her left and there was Emma, her heart-shaped face framed by a flattering elfin haircut, looking relaxed and lovely in a simple ivory gown softened by fluted sleeves and clever draping across her full bust. But it was the sight of Emma's father, walking proudly but so painfully slowly beside his daughter, that caused the tears in her eyes to spill over. Now, she recalled her dad mentioning that Emma had been busy ferrying her parents to hospital appointments, but it was evident from looking at the man so wasted by illness, his face grey and drawn with effort, that this would be one of the very last things he would ever do for his daughter. Small wonder that Emma's mother had been looking so worried.

Guy must have heard the sob that escaped her because she felt him place a protective arm round her waist. She took a deep breath and tried to steady herself. Guy was trying so hard, not only with her but with Wilma too, even volunteering to take the little dog for a walk to make sure she was comfortable before the ceremony. If she could just relax and loosen up a bit more with him and not worry too much about the double room her father had allocated them, she was sure everything would be fine.

Chloe watched as her dad and Emma faced each other for the first time, the look of love they exchanged was as if they were the only people there, yet it somehow lit the whole room. Would she ever feel that way about any man ever again? The tears rolled down her face as all the futile love and longing for Ryan flooded back. Guy pressed her closer to him and this time the sinews of her neck burned as she choked back her sobs. Guy was the smart choice; at heart he was a home bird, someone who was comfortable in the settled routine of domestic life, a backbone to support her when she needed him.

And for all her doubts about her father's remarriage, as the ceremony progressed and she witnessed her dad and his bride exchange their vows, she glimpsed a brighter, steadier future. So much of her childhood had been a precarious balancing act whilst she watched her mother's mood swings and tried to act as a counterweight to keep her on an even keel. Now she realised how much of a toll those years had taken on her father. Who could blame him for withdrawing into the shell of his study as the pendulum of her mother's moods veered to dangerous extremes? Who could fault him for seizing his chance of happiness and security?

Chloe reached for Guy's hand on her waist and held it tight. She vowed to try harder with him. Seeing the change in her father proved that lasting happiness required a firm foundation and a good partnership. Trying to hold on to someone who didn't want to be there, even with invisible ties woven from pure love, only led to misery.

★   ★   ★

Ryan started his climb at daybreak. By the time he reached the mountain summit, a strengthening wind tore at his hair. It was savagely cold too; bitter enough to make most people pull on a hat, but Ryan revelled in the feeling of freedom. This was the essence of his work; where others stayed behind their desks cocooned in their centrally-heated offices with only screen-savers to remind them of the outside world, he relished the challenge of breaking free, of losing himself in the wild landscape with its raw elemental forces.

The air was clear and sharp as crystal. He filled his lungs and felt the rhythm of his heart, still pounding after the exertions of the final steep ascent, steady as he slowly exhaled and took in the view. Sublime. He had no adequate words of his own to describe it, but the vocabulary of his camera work would, he hoped, express the sullen majesty of pewter pinnacles, corrie lakes like pools of mercury and a steely sky streaked with clouds of slate-grey.

He knew that a trough of low pressure was closing in fast. It was a calculation he'd made when he'd looked at the forecasts. Would it be damp and too misty to see any of the views at all, or could he seize a slim window of opportunity and capture the moody hues before the rain? His first thoughts about this assignment were based on better weather; sunlight gilding the blue-white of frost-covered slopes, iced grass that was brittle underfoot, gold reflections in the crackle-glazed streams, but he'd soon dismissed those ideas as clichés with all the longevity of a Christmas card. There wouldn't be anything cosy about today's work; this was nature untamed, bleak as the black rocky outcrops and free as the swooping buzzards. Why would anyone choose the claustrophobia of an office when there was a great big world to explore?

He glanced at his watch, although he didn't need to know the time to see that the light would fade fast, and tried not to think about Chloe. The wedding would be over by now, he hoped it hadn't been too difficult for her. The reception might even have begun, perhaps she was drinking a toast. With Guy. He shook his head. If Chloe thought Guy was right for her, then he was happy for her. Yet from everything she'd said about the man, he was pretty certain she was making a big mistake. Still, if she wanted the comforts of home and the security of a risk-averse lifestyle, she certainly wouldn't enjoy being buffeted by the icy wind at the top of Snowdon, nor would she fancy the descent and negotiating the fickle scree slope before the rain made it even more treacherous. No, she was better off without him, and he was better off alone, no dependents, free to come and go as he pleased.

His phone vibrated in his pocket and, as he fumbled to respond, he realised how cold his fingers had become. Although there hadn't been any signal on the way up, the fact that his phone had buzzed into life now was proof that reception really was as good as he'd heard it was supposed to be at the summit. The odds were that it was better than his signal at home in Little Spitmarsh. One day the town might even get high-speed broadband.

'Tansy?'

'Ryan! Are you down yet?'

He laughed at his cousin's faith in his speed.

'Hey, I'm good, but I'm not that fast.'

'I've been trying to call you.'

A stream of incoming messages

verified her words.

'I'm touched by your concern, but you know I'm fine. There's almost no signal anyway. What's up? You're not getting soft are you?' Then a thought occurred to him. 'Oh no, it's not Duncan is it? You two haven't broken up again, have you?'

He heard a muffled sob and knew he'd hit the nail on the head. Or perhaps Tansy had recovered her plastic spade and hit Duncan on the head. It really wasn't the time and place to be providing counselling and he was starting to feel the chill.

'What was it about this time?'

'It's not Duncan' she said, her voice faint. 'It's Fred. He's — '

'Tans! I can't hear you,' he shouted, praying for the violent gusts of wind sweeping the summit to ease so that he could listen. 'What's wrong with Fred?'

He hurled himself towards the lee of the closed visitor centre just as the swollen black clouds closing in on the mountain tore apart. 'Tans!'

9

Hopeless. Whatever Tansy was trying to say stuttered and fragmented as the signal dropped in and out. Vet? Had he heard correctly? Not 'dead', please not dead. Ryan punched at the screen to send a message and was hit by a low battery warning. Not possible. He swiped away the raindrops obscuring the glass. Five percent? Surely there was more left in the tank than that? Hadn't he recharged it during the journey? That had certainly been his intention, but the evidence suggested he'd been far too preoccupied to actually plug the damn thing in. So much for his hostile environment training. Not, of course, that he would ever be so stupid as to rely on a mobile phone to navigate a mountain, but now he had one fewer tool at his disposal in case of emergency and no fast way to find out exactly what condition Fred was in.

Ryan tried to stay calm by concentrating on the magnificence of the wild landscape. In any other circumstances, he would have relished being a solitary figure pitting himself against primordial forces. Now he wanted nothing more than to get down as fast as possible, reach his car and drive through the night if that's what it took to get to Tansy's. He tugged at his collar which was damp against his skin. The sly rain had crept round the visitor centre and was driving in hard and starting to bother him. His high-tech zip top had been good for the climb, but it wouldn't take long before he was soaked. He reached for his rucksack, glad of the streamlined waterproof jacket packed inside which would keep the worst of the weather at bay during what now looked like a tricky descent requiring all his concentration.

Except, he discovered, rummaging amongst food wrappers, packets of dried fruit, chocolate bars, spare cameras and bottles of water, there was no jacket.

Somehow he'd entirely missed packing it — along with his brains. And to think how scornful he'd been when he'd read about the stag party idiots who'd attempted to scale the mountain in a thunderstorm wearing only pyjamas. First rule of survival? Prepare for the environment and dress appropriately. His descent would, out of necessity, have to be painstaking and slow — a twisted ankle could mean hypothermia and with dark clouds now shrouding the mountain, there would be no rescue helicopter. Some poor sods would have to carry him down if he had an accident, assuming he didn't freeze to death while he was waiting.

In a rare moment of anger and frustration, Ryan nearly punched the nearest wall, but a broken hand wouldn't exactly speed things up. Instead, he took stock of what he did have; he pulled on the waterproof trousers, made a rudimentary cloak from his space blanket and gathered his thoughts. Now all he had to do was keep his wits about him as he made his descent. And hope that Fred, wherever he was, was hanging on.

* * *

'Do you want to see how Wilma's doing?' Guy asked when the seemingly endless round of photos was over. Chloe gave him a fond smile; thanks to his celebrity status he'd managed to persuade the hotel that one small, obedient dog would hardly be noticed by anyone if they were very discreet. Now, he even cared enough about Wilma to suggest checking on her without being prompted.

'I know I could do with a short break after all that emotion,' she replied. 'And I'm sure Dad and Emma won't even notice if we slip away for half an hour.'

Guy offered her his hand. People smiled at them as they moved through the guests and, as she caught sight of their reflection in one of the many large gilt-framed mirrors, she could see they made a glossy couple. Or was it because of Guy they were noticed? More people were beginning to recognise him since the move to national radio and although she could see it was very good for Guy's ego it made her feel even more like the lowly researcher and rather invisible.

'Is everything all right, sir?' A sultry waitress carrying glasses enquired, pouting at Guy, as they passed her on the way out. 'Perhaps sir would like another G&T?' she added, blatantly winking at him.

'Another?' Chloe arched an eyebrow at him? 'How many have you had?'

'Must be confusing me with someone else,' Guy muttered, hurrying Chloe along. Inside their livid yellow 'executive suite', she kicked off her shoes, poured more water out for an unusually quiet Wilma, then flopped back on the lavishly upholstered bed. The luxurious springs barely registered Guy's weight as he sat down beside her, loosened his tie and opened the top buttons of his shirt, but Chloe tensed when he stretched himself out next to her and ran his fingers up the inside of her thigh.

'Guy, I don't — '

'Hush,' he said, 'I know now is not the time, but you look so deliciously prim and proper that I've been having all sorts of fantasies about what you might be wearing underneath. But, listen, the last thing I want is to put you under pressure. I'm not naive — I know you had reservations when your dad and Emma jumped to conclusions and put us in the same room — and I want you to know that I'm willing to wait until you're ready. I've realised how important you are to me, how I've come to rely on you.'

Chloe made a dismissive gesture, but he caught hold of her hand. 'I'm serious, Chloe, and I've been doing some thinking. I want you in my life . . . '

He paused and took a deep breath. Chloe looked up as he started to frame the words and panicked about what she was going to hear. If he said he loved her, what then? And what if he'd caught wedding fever and was about to propose? How could she tell him it was too soon without hurting his feelings? He opened his lips and she took the only course of action she could think of, she threw her arms around his neck and kissed him. He pulled back, looking startled, then grinned and bent his head to kiss her throat.

Chloe closed her eyes whilst he moved his mouth slowly towards hers. Bittersweet sensations moved her; the warm familiarity of his endearingly respectful touch and the sad recognition that he would never be the man she wanted him to be. But he was the man who wanted her. She tried to shut out all other thoughts and give herself up to the moment which was made even harder by Wilma who had started making little yipping noises and scratching at the door.

Guy swore and dragged himself away. 'Your timing is really off, you know that, dog?' he said bearing down on Wilma.

'Guy, you don't need to raise your

voice,' she said quickly. 'She still isn't used to you and you'll scare her.'

'I know what I'm doing,' he insisted. 'She needs to learn the sound of her master's voice.'

'Oh for goodness sake, Guy.' Chloe sighed, realising that his voice was actually a little slurred, as if he'd needed more than one G&T to face the occasion. 'You're getting this out of all proportion. She'll be much more responsive to you if you calm down.'

'No,' he raised his hand in protest. 'You're too soft with her. By the way, I've decided she can stay in the kitchen when you visit. I'm not letting her near my carpets until she proves she can be trusted.'

'*What?*' Chloe leapt to her feet, but not in time to stop him scooping Wilma up by the scruff of her neck. 'That's enough, Guy,' she ordered. 'You're hurting her. Put her down immediately.'

'Don't tempt me,' Guy muttered, shrugging her off as she tried to take the terrified animal who was doing her utmost to fight back. 'For now I'm taking her over to the French doors to let her out for a pee.'

But not soon enough. The silence seemed to stretch out forever as they watched in horror as a dark stain started to spread across the front of Guy's light grey trousers. Guy swore and in his haste to put her down almost threw Wilma on the carpet where another wet patch pooled around the frightened dog.

'Now look what she's done!' he hissed. 'I didn't realise I was putting my reputation on the line for a vicious incontinent apology of an animal. You didn't warn me she'd trash the room!'

Chloe found she was shaking. 'Guy! Stop being so vile, Wilma never has accidents and she can certainly wait forty-five minutes so something's wrong.' She crouched down and Wilma, showing the whites of her eyes, slithered towards her and cowered under the shelf of her knees. Chloe stroked her gently, Wilma was terrified and trembling but didn't seem to be ill.

'Guy?' she asked, at last, when she could trust herself to speak. 'What do you mean 'vicious'? What happened when you walked her? You did take her for a walk before the ceremony, didn't you?'

'She went for me when I showed her the lead,' he said, rolling up a trouser leg and pointing to a non-existent scratch. 'So I shut her in the bathroom to cool down whilst I went off to have — '

'A G&T,' she finished for him.

The dark water and the four-legged creature. Now she understood why the fortune teller had been amused by his own prediction. One day, when she wasn't so furious and upset, she might see the funny side of how the prophecy had unfolded too. But for now she didn't need anyone to reveal the identity of the man who was about to disappear from her future.

'Guy,' she said firmly. 'Pack your things and go right now. It's over.'

* * *

Every wretched stretch of the long drive from Snowdonia to Little Spitmarsh threw another obstacle in Ryan's way. Tansy had been able to reassure him, once he'd got enough juice in his phone to ring her, that Fred wasn't in any immediate danger, but the possible slipped disc he was being investigated for might cause long-term damage. All Ryan wanted was to be at the poor basset's side.

The heavy rain was causing havoc all along the route; a flooded lane meant a tortuous diversion through winding roads then a long delay at temporary traffic lights. He'd barely got past that holdup when the traffic ground to a halt again and he found himself in lengthy tailback which, he eventually found out, was due to a car skidding off the wet road. Inching past the flashing lights of emergency vehicles attending the scene, hoping no one was seriously hurt, only a heightened sense of caution and telling himself that the painkillers prescribed by the vet had made his poor hound more comfortable stopped him putting his foot down to compensate for lost time.

Bloody Vic and Bob! If Tansy's evil twin cats hadn't been tormenting poor Fred, he wouldn't have launched himself at the top of the sofa trying to get to them. It was obvious to him they'd been offloaded on to the local cat protection team because their sadistic personalities were too much for the previous owner. If Tansy hadn't been such a bleeding heart and taken them in, Fred wouldn't be facing the possibility of life-changing injuries.

At last his headlights picked up a familiar road sign; three miles to go. Ryan yawned, his anger and concern only blunted by extreme fatigue. The descent from Snowdon had been tricky in the poor light and his muscles burned from bracing himself on wet, slippery scree. He blinked hard, trying to refresh eyes that were sore from concentrating on the oily roads in a downpour that had followed him every step of a mile. His head was pounding, as if his skull was about to split and he realised how foolhardy it was to have driven so far without a break. Nevertheless, it was only by taking action that he could shut out the voice inside telling him that the only person he ought to be blaming for Fred's accident was himself.

Fred wasn't getting any younger. As much as Ryan loved having him along with him on his shoots, practicalities were forcing him to leave his beloved dog behind more frequently. If Fred's injured back didn't repair properly there was a real possibility he wouldn't be travelling at all. What then? Ryan relished the freedom of being able to take off when and wherever he liked, but was it fair to abandon Fred if he became housebound? And even if Tansy was willing to help, there was still the problem of Vic and Bob. He didn't doubt that there were solutions to be found, people trained to dog-sit, but would Fred understand? Heaven knows, if his girlfriends had grown a little cold every time he left them behind, how could he expect a dog to know that it was only for short periods, not forever?

In his mind's eye he saw Chloe, her dark eyes lighting up as he walked through their door. Would he be so keen to leave if she was there to welcome him when he came home? Then he looked a little further into the future and imagined a wife and baby; a wife who would surely grow increasingly resentful when burdened with the entire weight of parenting. He shook his throbbing head as Tansy's little cottage came into view. Parking carefully, he put the handbrake on, rubbed his hands across his face as if to erase the exhaustion and tried to peer through the dark shrubs obscuring the front bay window. Hard to see if anyone was still awake.

He climbed out on stiff legs, draped a coat over his shoulder to keep off the worst of the rain and headed for the front door. Gusty wind shook the branches of the shrubs, sounding eerily wild and animate as it died away. Before him, the house was in darkness, except for a light in the hall. Ryan tapped the knocker and waited. Just as he was about to give it a thump a pool of light spilled out from somewhere above him and a few minutes later he could make out, through the obscure glazing, a shape moving towards him.

Perhaps it was because time dragged impossibly slowly whilst Tansy fumbled to unlock the door, that he barely registered the eerie yowling swelling to a crescendo just behind him or the hissing and spitting in the bushes beside him. Any moment now and he would know exactly how Fred was doing; he couldn't wait to see his old mate. Tansy opened the door, her orange corkscrew curls dishevelled, accentuating the pallor of her worried face.

'Ryan, thank God. It's okay, don't panic. Fred's as comfortable as can be expected. Come in and I'll tell you all about it.'

He released the breath he'd been holding and took a step forwards. 'Boy, am I glad to see you,' he told her just as two dark shapes shot out the bushes and launched themselves towards the doorway. 'What the?' he began, completely disorientated. With his foot in mid-air, the world spinning and an indignant bundle of writhing, clawing energy taking up the exact same space he was aiming for, there was nowhere to go except down. Ryan snatched at the air in vain as the ground disappeared under his feet.

10

Halfway down her third glass of Prosecco, Chloe decided that she quite liked the Baroque vibe of the hotel's wedding reception room with its turquoise walls and lashings of gold detailing. What wasn't there to love about a fat, gilt decorative cherub or three? She felt surprisingly okay to be standing there on her own. More than okay, in fact, she was getting better by the minute, positively light-headed, you could say. It had taken a little while to reassure Wilma that she was safe, but eventually the little dog had fallen into a sound sleep on a spare duvet Chloe had acquired from reception by telling the receptionist that Guy Bradshaw was liable to wet the bed if he got too cold. Even the thought of Guy made her shudder; she was so, so relieved to have found out in the nick of time, that although *some* big beasts thought they could borrow a pussy cat's disguise, leopards *never* changed their spots.

'I haven't seen Guy for a little while,' said Emma, looking worried beside her. 'Is everything all right?'

'Fine,' Chloe said, nodding. Damn it, she was not going to let anything cast a cloud over the happy couple's perfect day. Some couples had to be happy. If Emma made her dad happy, the least she could do was paste on a cheerful smile and be happy for him. 'Actually,' she said, grabbing Emma's arm to pull her a bit closer, 'it's his incontinence.'

'Guy?' Emma's eyebrows rose then fell.

Chloe swapped her empty glass for a full one as an obliging waiter went past. She leaned forward to grab Emma again and, luckily, only spilled a few drops of Prosecco down the bride. 'Whoops! Just a dribble! Not like Guy, bless him,' she went on in a stage-whisper. 'No spare trousers, unfortunately.'

'Oh poor man,' Emma said, stepping

back. 'What a shame! I'm sure everyone here would understand, but it must be so embarrassing for him.'

Chloe nodded, then reminded herself to take all movements more slowly. 'That's why he does radio,' she said solemnly.

'Chloe, are you sure you're okay?' Emma said, her brows furrowing. 'I know today can't be the easiest for you, especially now you're without an escort — '

'Pah! Who needs a man?' Chloe swung her arm and unintentionally sent a nearby fascinator flying. 'Obviously you do, because you've just got married. And,' she added quickly seeing Emma's face fall. 'That's lovely. Good for you. And good for me, because I now have a brand new stepmother.'

'Really?' Tears gathered in Emma's eyes. 'I've been so worried, Chloe. I know I can't take your mother's place, and I'd never try to, but I do want us to be friends.'

'Of course, we'll be friends!' Chloe accidentally left Rouge Allure on

Emma's cheek when she planted a kiss on her but managed to scrub it off with the edge of her cover-up.

'Thank you,' Emma said with a watery smile. 'Look, your dad's calling me over. I'd better go over, we're going to have a couple of short informal speeches then we'll open the evening buffet. It might be a good idea to have something to eat, don't you think?'

But Chloe wasn't listening. 'Speeches?' she said. 'Great! I'll say a few words!'

★   ★   ★

'Darling, are you sure you want to do this?' said Chloe's dad, after everyone had listened, smiling, to the lovely thoughts he shared about Emma becoming his wife. Chloe put her empty glass next to the cake which was topped by little fondant effigies of her dad carrying Emma in his arms. 'Have you secretly been going to the gym, Dad?' she asked, guffawing. 'You'll never get Emma over the threshold otherwise.

Not,' she added, seeing Emma's bottom lip quiver and a look in the eyes of the mother of the bride that suggested she might pick up a cake knife and slaughter her if she didn't make amends very quickly, 'that I'm suggesting no one could lift Emma, because Emma is, that is, she has a lovely curvy figure and looks truly beautiful today. No, what I meant is that all you do is sit at a desk all day, Dad, and you're a lot older than Emma so perhaps she'd better carry you.'

Stoney faces all round suggested she was never going to make it as a stand-up comedienne. Chloe flapped her top about a bit to give herself some air as it was suddenly very hot in the room. In doing so she had a feeling she might have flashed one of the male guests who grinned and winked at her. Cheeky git, she thought, what would Ryan have said to him? Had Ryan been there, she wouldn't have needed a couple of medicinal drinks to get through the day. She wouldn't have invited Guy in the first place then *he* wouldn't have behaved so monstrously towards Wilma. If Ryan had been there, she wouldn't be in this mess at all. But Ryan probably wasn't even sparing her a second thought and however wretched she felt, however much she missed him, this was not the moment to crawl under the buffet table and howl. She took a deep breath.

'Sorry,' she said quietly, 'let me start again. When Dad first told me he'd met someone, I was pleased because I hated the thought of him being on his own for the rest of his life. 'Someone' was fine in theory because, without specifics, I could carry on believing nothing would change, you know? It was still just me, Dad and Mum's memory. Even when Dad introduced me to Emma, I chose not to see how important she was to him. It came as a shock when Dad proposed to Emma; I felt as if he was moving on and leaving me and Mum behind and I resented it.'

Oh God, the look on everyone's

faces! She could see the spoilt brat she'd been reflected in their eyes.

'Yes, Dad is moving on and if anyone deserves a second chance at happiness, he does. We both loved my mum very much, but her illness made it very difficult at times, especially for Dad who shielded me from the worst and carried the biggest burden of her care.'

Now she was depressing the hell out of everyone.

'To be completely honest, I still wasn't sure if Dad was doing the right thing until today. At today's ceremony, I looked at my father and saw a man I almost didn't recognise. Someone looking forwards to his future, freed from the responsibilities of the past. I will never, ever forget the joy and love on his face when he saw Emma, looking so beautiful, as she walked towards him. I saw how much my dad loves Emma and that his love is reciprocated by a very special lady. Thank you, Emma. I couldn't be happier for you both. Ladies and gentlemen, please raise your glasses to the bride and groom!'

Chloe was about to reach for her empty glass but someone thoughtfully handed her a full one; the guest she had flashed had somehow turned up by her side. They toasted the happy couple then, as the group of guests dispersed, he steered her towards the buffet, loaded two plates and found them somewhere to sit.

'Chloe, isn't it?'

She eyed him over her glass. Ordinary, pleasant-looking man. Not flamboyant like Guy nor wild like Ryan.

'Ben,' he supplied, along with another cheeky grin. 'Great speech!'

Chloe would have been more inclined to believe him if he'd been addressing her face not her breasts. She sipped her drink whilst she thought about it. Perhaps he was just shy and needed to warm up?

'Thank you, Ben,' she tried to say, except it came out a bit slurred. 'Nice to meet you.'

'And you,' he said, leaning closer so

that his legs brushed hers. 'To new friends.'

'New friends!' she declared raising her glass. Nice to have a new friend. But as he chinked his glass to hers, he made the mistake of revealing the wedding band on his left hand. Not so nice to have a friend who was a cheat, she decided, and slowly let the contents of her glass trickle into his lap. Whilst he was still in shock, Chloe made hasty excuses to her dad and Emma, quickly waving away their concerns and the troubled looks they were exchanging so that she could beat a winding path to her room. Wilma, once assured that the dreadful man who had frightened her so much was nowhere in sight, greeted her with much wagging of her tail and loving licks. Since puppyhood, she'd always been very good about making her needs clear, and the stain on the carpet was barely noticeable now, but to be on the safe side before they retired for the night, Chloe opened the French doors to let Wilma out and sank down in the doorway to let the cold drizzly breeze clear her thumping head.

Life could be very unfair, she decided, playing with her phone. None of this would have happened if Ryan had been with her. She had a good mind to tell him so, in fact, why not let him know this minute? She thought about what she was going to say whilst the number dialled and was so disappointed when it went to voicemail that she felt compelled to try again. Much better. That would tell him. Although had she really got everything off her chest? Airing her grievances was making her very tired, though, and she was getting cold so she signed off with one more garbled message and killed the call. Goodness, her head was hurting. What she really needed to do was go to bed. She stood up warily as, for all the cold air rushing in, the room had started spinning. As she went to close the doors, she realised something wasn't right. Where was Wilma?

11

Ryan sank back slowly into the familiar embrace of his battered leather arm-chair and tried to work out why it didn't feel better to be back in his own home. He closed his eyes, his exhausted body reaching for the obvious solution of sleep when his doorbell chimed and Tansy coo-eed from the hall at him. There was a double thud as she kicked off her chunky boots before bursting into the sitting room, the cold air still clinging to her.

'Hey, Frankenstein, you made it down-stairs. You were still asleep when I called round first thing. How does it feel to be up and about?' she asked, dropping a kiss on his cheek as she unwound a scarlet scarf strung with multicoloured felt bobbles from her vivid orange coat.

Ryan ran very tentative fingertips over the staples on the back of his head.

'It'll be better when these things are removed.'

'Only a couple of days now,' she said, pushing him forwards to have a look. 'The cut's healing really well though. And the hair will grow back . . . '

They eyed each other ruefully as she flopped down opposite him.

'When I first came round, I thought . . . ' He struggled to control his emotions. 'I thought what had happened to Pa was happening to me. I was afraid I'd had a stroke.'

Tansy gave a great shuddering breath. '*You* were scared. I thought you were dead. Good job you've got such a thick skull eh? I thought at first that Vic and Bob had finished you off when you hit the deck and didn't get up.'

'I might finish them off when I've got my strength up,' he told her, only half-joking.

'That's what you told the paramedics when you came round. They were getting ready to call the police until I explained Vic and Bob were cats.'

'They're not cats, they're fiends!' he said with feeling. He was about to expand on his theme when the doorbell chimed again.

'That'll be Duncan,' Tansy said, her expression softening as she went to answer the door. Ryan wasn't used to feeling sorry for himself, but his cousin's happiness only made him realise how lonely and dull the next few days would be, giving him far too long to think about everything he regretted.

Tansy had lit a fire earlier yet the cheery crackling sound only contrasted with the sudden emptiness of the room. Vast open spaces never bothered him when he was out on a shoot; the wilder the environment, the more he enjoyed the challenge. It showed in his work, in the photographs which brought him a decent living, a fair amount of prize money and professional acclaim.

Being able to stand his own company, he reminded himself as he looked around, had earned him enough money to invest in a property, albeit in the largely unknown seaside resort of Little Spitmarsh whose economic tide still drifted between ebb and flow. Buyers in Highgate would have been fighting over the shabby Victorian villa, but in Little Spitmarsh they were so thin on the ground he'd picked it up for what almost anywhere else in the country would have been a laughable sum for a property barely ten minutes away from a stunning waterway.

One of its attractions for him was having his fierce and deeply loyal cousin nearby and it wasn't a bad run to his parents in Norwich where his dad had worked as an actuary until he suffered the stroke that had such devastating effects on all their lives. He ran his fingers over his scalp again as he realised how fortunate he'd been. For years he'd secretly worried that he might be harbouring an inherent genetic weakness from his father that might one day prevent him doing all the things he loved. Worse still, he dreaded the thought of being a burden to someone who loved him. In the early months after his father's stroke, his mother had stepped in to take care of every aspect of his father's personal needs and did it all without complaint. Ryan remained horrified by the idea of being so utterly dependent, yet a stupid accident might equally have left him with a life-changing head injury. He was beginning to realise that after years of worrying about something that might never happen, he'd been very lucky to escape from his fall with staples and an overnight observation in Great Spitmarsh General Hospital before being pronounced fit to go home.

Ryan leaned back slowly. He had every reason to be grateful, yet he still had the feeling that something was missing. When his eyelids closed, he replayed the same scenes; Chloe walking away from him and a windscreen blurred with rain as he drove through the night to get to Fred. Chloe was gone and he hated to think how close he'd come to losing Fred too.

Gradually he became aware that the voices in his hall had dropped to a hush. What now? He heard footsteps on the gravel drive, a car door closing, a dull thump as the front door swung back against the hall wall and then a low whine that didn't sound anything like Duncan.

'Fred!'

When the basset lumbered over and laid his big head on Ryan's knee, all the pent up feeling he'd been holding back burst to the surface. A lump in his throat rendered him speechless and it was as much as he could do to stop the tears falling.

'It's good news,' Tansy said, not helping him at all because her tears were flowing freely. 'It was a very severe muscle spasm, not a slipped disc. The vet's scrutinised the results to confirm that there's no serious underlying damage. He's sent Fred home with more medication just in case he's in pain.'

'And the future?' Ryan asked, knowing in his heart that Fred was only going to become more fragile with age.

Tansy managed a watery smile. 'For now, he'll get better with a good diet and plenty of rest. In the longer term, he'll need to avoid mountain-climbing and sofa-hurdling. There's a weakness in his back which means that next time he might not escape so lightly.'

Duncan looked round the door at them, breaking the heavy silence that fell between them. 'Okay to come in?'

Duncan never seemed to alter to Ryan, who could remember him as a little boy when Duncan's family used to rent the beach hut next door to the one owned by their great-uncle Sidney. His frank, open face always wore a slightly worried expression. No wonder, with Tans keeping him on his toes all the time. Ryan waved him in, but Duncan withdrew only to return with a rather splendid corduroy-covered mattress which he laid on the floor beside Ryan. 'Memory foam dog bed,' he explained.

'It's a present from Bob and Vic to say sorry to Fred and so that the pair of you can convalesce in comfort together,' Tansy added as Fred, abandoning Ryan's knee, arranged himself on the mattress with an expression of doggy bliss.

Ryan rubbed his eyes before any tell-tale tears fell and brushed a hand across his face, noting that his beard was threatening to run rampant if he didn't trim it soon. He looked at Tansy and Duncan standing there hand-in-hand, at Fred at his feet and felt a much happier man, except for one thing. 'When are you going to let me have my phone and laptop?'

Tansy shook her head. 'I'm not. Not today anyway. When you can tell me honestly that your headache's gone you can have them back but not before.' A sly smile lifted the corners of her mouth. 'Unless that blow to the head has knocked some sense into you and you want to call Chloe, then I could make an exception.'

'Stop trying to match-make, Tans. It's too late. Chloe doesn't need someone like me.'

'Tansy let go of Duncan's hand, walked over and dropped down beside him. 'Someone who really cares about her, you mean. Someone who contrived some crazy plan to go all the way to Hong Kong to show her how important she is to him. Someone who'd rather face a night on the bare mountain than confront his feelings. Come on, Ryan, you can't run away from your emotions forever.'

'*My* emotions aren't the issue here,' he said, feeling a band of tension tighten across his aching head. 'I can't give Chloe what she wants. Besides, you know me. Work will always come first, so give me my phone and laptop and let me get back to it.'

A smile had never faded so fast, thought Ryan. Or changed to something so full of murderous intent.

'Ryan Green,' Tansy said, almost breathing fire. 'If you're determined to put yourself in danger again there's nothing I can do to stop you, but if Fred comes to any harm because of your pig-headedness, I guarantee you won't need to go back to hospital to have those staples removed because I will personally remove them one by one. *With my tweezers!*

Since Tansy looked as if she was tempted to carry out her threat anyway, just for the hell of it, Ryan was especially grateful when the doorbell chimed for a third time. Everyone shot puzzled looks at each other before Duncan went off to answer the door. Then the room was filled with voices and laughter and he was enveloped in a cloud of Miss Dior as his mother wrapped her arms around him.

In his weakened state, Ryan was struck by how normal his parents looked — much better than him, in fact. Apart from the slight droop on the left side of his father's face and the walking stick he relied upon, it wasn't immediately apparent that there was anything wrong. In his slim-fitting jeans and trendy cashmere sweater, he cut a very different figure to the forlorn, frightened man he'd been in the early days after his stroke, when the doctors warned the family he probably wouldn't make it. No one looking at his youthful, pretty mother either, with her ash-blonde highlights and trim figure, could imagine the heartache she'd suffered or the battles she'd faced to get his father to where he was today. Nevertheless he was still bothered about them.

'Ma, Pa — there was absolutely no need to come all this way. Pa, it's too tiring for you.'

'Will you just stop fretting, Ryan, and let me be the judge of what I can and can't do,' his dad interrupted, shaking his head. 'One day, you're going to have to accept that I'm no longer a patient, I'm a stroke *survivor*. And I'm bloody grateful for the life I've got. So for once, will you shut up and let us take care of you! I'm not the invalid here, you are!'

★   ★   ★

When Chloe opened her eyes and stretched out for her phone she was pleased to see that her arm had stopped shaking. Everything looked reassuringly normal. Winter light streamed in through the Velux windows of her attic bedroom. A cosy tartan throw, draped over the foot of the bed, kept her snug. Even Wilma looked contrite. So it was a bit of a shock, when she checked, to find that it was now the third morning after the colourful night of her dad's wedding. The forty-eight hours or so of shivering and shaking with what felt like The Cold From The Black Lagoon had passed in a blur whilst she dragged herself from the bedroom down to the kitchen to feed Wilma or dose up on hot lemon medication before taking herself back to bed again.

She sat up, feeling slightly more human, and put out a hand which Wilma graciously sniffed before giving it a delicate lick — which Chloe took as the nearest thing to an apology for leading her on a merry dance — then commenced her energy-saving slither further along the duvet to sink down beside Chloe with a small sigh as if the effort had been too much for her.

Chloe lay back and stared at the painted white beams above her head. Everything would be lovely, she decided, if she could just stay cocooned in the gentle world of her two rooms at the top of her dad and stepmother's home. That way she could pretend that the embers of the spectacular nosedive her life had just taken weren't still smouldering all around her.

At least the hotel had decided not to press for damages which she had a strong suspicion was more to do with Guy's celebrity status — even though it was entirely Guy's fault that Wilma had scratched the back of the door because she was so desperate to get out. And he was *definitely* to blame for her peeing on the floor. Arguably he was also responsible for frightening Wilma so badly that for all Chloe's reassurances, she'd still fled into the hotel grounds, prepared to take her chances there rather than risk another encounter with the evil monster.

Goodness what a performance that had been! The sudden downpour had at least cleared Chloe's throbbing head enough for her to scour the gardens looking for Wilma. It was fortunate that with the wedding party disco in full swing no one else had heard her shouting her head off like a crazy woman. After all that crawling around on her hands and knees it had been a great relief to find Wilma sheltering under a shrub just outside the French doors. It was just a pity that Chloe hadn't thought to brush the mud off either of them before she'd stomped back in, collapsed on the bed and gone out like a light until a chambermaid opened the door, long after the other wedding guests had departed the next day, and found them.

She hadn't planned to rush back to the hotel any time soon, so being banned from their premises for life wasn't such a big deal, although she probably ought to own up to Emma and her dad when they returned from their honeymoon cruise just in case there were any unpleasant repercussions. Hopefully another twelve days would be sufficient time for the worst of the aftermath to blow over . . .

A fit of coughing forced her to sit up again, to Wilma's obvious irritation, but she no longer felt that the slightest movement might cause her to spontaneously combust. She prayed that whatever bug had invaded her was losing interest, but it had been a rough couple of days. There wasn't going to be a 'next time' so she didn't need to remind herself to put on a coat in future before wandering round in the freezing rain with the mother of all hangovers. No wonder her immune system had taken a pounding. All things considered, she'd got off lightly. For now she could simply shut out the world and recover at her own pace and without anyone fussing over her.

Except there was no longer anyone to fuss over her, she realised as she scanned her phone again. A short text from her dad and Emma let her know they'd reached their cruise ship in Tenerife safely and would phone her from their travels as soon as their schedule permitted. She flicked a quick glance at her emails where there was nothing of note except the one from the HR department informing her that she would not be offered a contract at the end of three month probationary period and explaining that, although she would be paid, she was not required to come into work.

Chloe read it twice. Well, that was something; now she didn't even need to go to the bother of handing in her resignation. Since she hadn't received or signed any paperwork or paid a deposit on the sterile modern flat Guy had found, she supposed that offer had also been withdrawn which was quite a relief. Trying to envisage herself living there had depressed her from the start, but now she wanted to be as far away from Guy as possible. The thought of how misguided she'd been to think he was offering her security and stability made her feel sick. How could she have been taken in twice by a man who loathed Wilma so much he'd been physically cruel to her? What would his adoring public think if they knew the truth behind the oh so caring voice?

Chloe swung her legs out of bed, eliciting a small moan of protest from Wilma. Then reality hit, sending her temperature soaring. She would leave it to fate to deal with Guy, but in the meantime he still had a job whereas she was left with a scant three months' salary to live on. She fanned her face as the enormity of being unemployed sank in. Unless she got her act together very quickly she'd be reduced to living in her parents' loft for the rest of her life. She pushed a hand through her hair which badly needed washing and was glad there was no one to see the mess she was in.

She staggered to her feet and was about to head for the bathroom when something about being in a mess disturbed another memory which she must have tried to bury. Biting her lip, she scrolled through her phone again and found the history of her drunk-dialling Ryan. The room swayed and stars exploded in her vision as fresh waves of humiliation crashed over her. Which was worse, she wondered, that she sent increasingly tearful messages to Ryan asking him why hehadn't been there for her when she needed him? Or that Ryan had simply ignored her?

Steadying herself against the door, Chloe waited for her face to cool down. A nano-second earlier the prospect of sharing a loft with a flatulent dachshund for the foreseeable future seemed desperately tragic. Now she was ready to bar the door against all-comers and live on takeaways for the rest of her life. When was the best time to tell her dad and Emma that it would be three of them in their new marriage, she wondered? Rather than making her fresh new start in the big city, she had become a boomerang child, doomed to arrive back at her place of origin instead of successfully flying the nest. If only the banging in her head would stop so she could think clearly. Frowning, Chloe realised that the banging seemed to be coming from somewhere oddly close to the front door. What on earth was going on?

Grabbing her phone and a dressing-gown, she hurried down two sets of stairs ready to report any lurking vandals to the police and opened the door only to hear a van driving away. The prestigious suburban street had returned to its usual state of leafy calm. Only one thing had changed; a 'for sale' board had been boldly planted in her dad's neat front garden.

12

As the room swam, Ryan resisted a sudden urge to lean back and let his head rest against the attractive auburn-haired nurse's white coat. For all his hostile environment training he was useless with anything to do with needles and had been dreading the moment the five staples were removed from his head wound.

'Last one,' the nurse said, as he felt a sharp sting. 'Would you like them as souvenirs?'

Tempting as it was to offer them to Tansy, there was a good chance she might withhold his phone and laptop permanently if he did.

'Do you need to sit here for a little while? You're looking quite pale,' the nurse said, surveying him with concern in her wide green eyes. It was true that he felt light-headed, but then again he'd lost a considerable weight of hair and a dense beard. Small wonder his face looked pale when it had been hiding in the undergrowth for so long.

'I'll be fine,' he replied, standing up cautiously, 'and I'm getting a lift home.'

'Good. Just try not to have any slips or falls over the next few weeks,' she said, with the hint of a smile. 'It looks nice and clean, but pop back to the surgery if you're worried at all and I'll have another look at you.'

Wouldn't it be nice, he thought as he thanked her and left the room, if it was as easy as that? How simple it would be if the lovely nurse could kiss all his hurts better, but there was no prescription for his aching heart.

Tansy, in the waiting room, frowned when she caught sight of him.

'What's wrong now?' he asked as they stepped out into sleety rain.

'It's a bit of a shock finding out that you're quite good-looking underneath all that hair,' she said, pointing him towards her car. 'Just mind how you go on this slippery pavement. We don't want you spoiling that pretty face now you've rediscovered it, do we?'

Ryan reminded himself that he only had to be polite to Tansy for another fifteen minutes until they were back at his house where Duncan was looking after Fred as his parents had theatre tickets for a play they were keen to see.

'You know it did me good to see Ma and Pa outside their usual environment,' he mused. 'For years, I though Ma had had the worst luck of all, having to nurse Pa through his rehabilitation and yet . . . '

'And yet their relationship is warmer and closer than ever,' Tansy finished for him. 'You know that vow they made? 'In sickness and in health', that makes them a team, right? It means pulling together through thick and thin, not bailing out when you realise you've fallen in love *in case* something goes wrong.'

She shot him a look before edging out of the car park. Ryan kept his mouth shut but all bets were off once he was reunited with his phone and laptop.

'You're going to need a thermal hat for the next mountain,' she muttered disapprovingly as she negotiated her way through the winding roads.

The windscreen wipers were having trouble keeping up in the appalling conditions so he waited until they were back inside to talk to her. Once he'd reassured himself that Fred was still in one piece and everyone was sitting down with fresh coffee, Tansy opened her bag and reluctantly returned his precious links to the outside world.

'I still think you're being totally irresponsible,' she said, shooting daggers at him with her eyes.

'Really? Tell me what you think a group of octogenarians are going to do to me?' Ryan grinned seeing Tansy and Duncan both wearing the same shocked expressions and leaned back in his chair feeling like a conjuror who'd just produced a Flemish Giant rabbit out of a miniature top hat.

'My next assignment is a birthday party and now I can firm up the arrangements. Heck, I've even smartened up for the occasion,' he added, pointing to his hair. 'Admittedly, the hospital gave me a bit of a head-start with that, although I don't think much of their stylist. What happened was that when I was on the ward, I got talking to an elderly chap in the bed next to me. Charlie. He'd been brought in from a care home in Great Spitmarsh after a fall, nothing too serious but they wanted to rule out any underlying causes. It turned out that it's Charlie's birthday next week. He's ninety so when one of the carers came in to get the results of Charlie's tests I asked if I could go in to the home to take some photographs to mark the occasion.'

'But Ryan, you've never gone down the portrait route,' Tansy said, raising her eyebrows, 'you're always trying to get away from people.'

Ryan shrugged. Was he *that* anti-social? 'I've covered enough personal interest stories with news and sports items. It just seemed an obvious way to give the poor old sod a bit of boost. Think about it, ninety years which have spanned wars, recession and real hardship, but on a personal level, a life well-led, a country served, a wife loved and lost. Who else is going to be there for him? Everyone Charlie loved is dead, and the only friends he has are in the care home and some of them barely know their own names.'

Talking to the old man, he decided to keep to himself, had also shown him an unwelcome glimpse of the future. One where he didn't have the luxury of choosing solitude, but of having it thrust upon him. No one decided to be lonely.

'And of course, there's Fred. I'm not going to do anything that will put him at risk, but he's not going to understand when I leave him behind. The mountain commission's out now so I might as well make myself useful while I decide what my next project will be. The carer at Charlie's home says there aren't enough volunteers willing to help the old folks break the monotony and, with permission, Fred can come along too and cheer up the residents who miss their pets.'

'Wow!' Tansy shook her head in disbelief. 'That's quite a step. What are you going to do for an income?'

'Tans, I'm freelance, I've never had what you could call job security. Something will turn up, it always does. I'll just have to pick my commissions carefully. I might even start doing weddings — what do you think?'

He glanced up to find Tansy giving him a shrewd stare. 'I don't suppose there's another reason why you've suddenly decided mountain-climbing's a bit risky, is there? Perhaps there's someone else who'd like you to stay closer to home? Maybe that's why you've started thinking about weddings.'

'I promise you I've no plans to propose to anyone any time soon,' he reassured her, forcing a smile. 'Besides, who'd have me? I've lost my beard, my income and I come with a dependent old dog. Of course, if you and Duncan fancy a trip down the aisle, it would be my great pleasure to compile the wedding album to you as my gift.'

Now it was Tansy's turn to look nervous. He chuckled to himself as she suddenly seemed anxious to get Duncan to his feet and out the door. Deep down she was far more of a commitment-phobe than him.

'But before we go,' she said bearing down on him. 'I think it's time I checked your temperature. If the nurse hadn't given you a clean bill of health, I'd say you were suffering from extremely delayed concussion. Wedding photography, ha ha! That *will* be the day!'

She stuck a thermometer under his tongue before Ryan could say another word then made it worse by leaning in and whispering, 'I know you, Ryan Green. I know it's easier for you to let the camera do the talking for you, but sometimes you have to spell it out. You'll never know what Chloe's true feelings are until you reveal yours. Give her a chance, Ryan. Tell her.'

He let her kiss him goodbye then sat back and waited until he heard the car drive away before picking up his phone. Thinking about weddings generally gave him a bad feeling, but especially now. What if wedding fever *had* struck and Chloe *had* done something really stupid like getting engaged to Guy? Would sending her the ten photos he'd promised her from their trip to Hong Kong bring bad news in return? He eyed his phone warily, took a deep breath and saw that he had missed five calls, all within a fifteen minute slot, all from Chloe. Either she was really, really happy about that engagement. Or he hadn't been there for her when she really needed to speak to him.

* * *

Chloe pounced gratefully on her phone when it rang. Three days after posting her CV online and out to as many agencies and employers she could think of, she was starting to get paranoid about the lack of response. She'd clocked up plenty of experience for sure, but her skill-set didn't fit neatly into the formal boxes prospective employers expected her to fill. Pinning all her career hopes on Guy had been fine when the going was good, but now she was faced with the frightening prospect of having to prove herself all over again. Moreover, it had been years since she'd actively tried to find work and there were far more fish in the radio researcher pond, many of them eager to swallow the hook of minimal wages or very short-term contracts in a cannibalistic feeding frenzy for which she had no appetite.

She cleared her throat before answering the call in an effort to find a phone voice which exuded eminent employability. After days of making conversation with no one except Wilma, which was a bit one-sided, the result was weaker than she'd have liked, but in any case her efforts were thwarted by the disconcerting sound of whistles, drums and what sounded like a carnival going on in the offices of whoever was trying to call her.

'Chloe? Is that you?'

'Dad? Where are you?'

'Sorry my darling, I can't hear you very well. Believe it or not, we're at a carnival in Mindelo. We're having the most wonderful time! Actually, I'm rather enjoying all this partying. When Emma and I come to visit you in London, you might have to take us clubbing!'

Chloe squeezed her eyes shut in an effort to erase the terrifying vision her dad had just seared on her brain. Fortunately she had enough energy left to clamp her hand over her mouth before she blurted out the awful truth about being unemployed and almost homeless too.

'You're happy then,' she said weakly when she could trust herself to speak.

'Happier than I've ever been!' her dad replied against a peal of laughter in the background. 'You know, darling, before I could never understand the meaning of that expression about not being here for a long time but for a good time, but now I do. I'm so fortunate to have found Emma. I feel as if I've been given a second chance at life. We've decided to make a fresh start all round starting off with selling both our houses and buying something to call our own. I left the keys with the agent before we went away so they can show people round at any time. Probably should have mentioned it to you sooner but with the wedding and your holiday I never quite got round to it. Besides, you're up and away with your career, your man and your London pad so we're all sorted. Anyway, darling, we'll catch up properly when we get back. Have fun!'

Have fun? Chloe set her phone down and buried her head in her hands. She wasn't even aware that her father knew what fun was. As for her dry, academic old dad going through his moves with carnival queens in sequinned bikinis, it was just too bizarre to think about. From nowhere, a dry bubble of laughter rose up inside her and once she started to laugh, it was difficult to stop. The thought that at any moment an estate agent could open the door to show potential buyers round the property only to find her sitting there, still in her pyjamas at midday, eating peanut butter toast whilst morosely perusing the job adverts on her laptop had her clutching her sides and hooting even more.

Could anyone have predicted that after all her fears for her father, all the years she'd spent close to his side, trying in a small way to fill the emptiness her mother had left in both their lives, that *he* would be the one to shake himself up, find a partner, marry and build a new future? And what, a small, resentful voice inside asked, did *she* have to look forward to? Had she really given up so many opportunities for this? She wasn't exactly sure where a degree in psychology might have taken her, but she certainly wouldn't have wasted so much time making tea for her dad or Guy.

For a moment, the unfairness of it all overwhelmed her until she began to realise that no one had forced her to stay at home, no one had made her work for Guy. The truth was that even if she'd completed her degree she probably would have chosen the safe and easy route because deep down she was afraid of risk, scared of failure and frightened of being hurt. She wrapped her arms around herself, leaning forwards as she admitted that the only person she could blame for her current situation was herself. It was only when Wilma dragged herself out of the bed in front of the Aga and stood up to rest her paws on Chloe's knees that she noticed the fat teardrops plopping onto her toast and realised she was crying.

'Oh Wilma,' she sobbed, wiping her nose on her sleeve, before stroking the little dachshund's soft head. 'Do you remember that evening when we sat at the water's edge and I wished on a star? I should have wished for the courage to take chances.'

She reached down and drew Wilma onto her lap, knocking her keyboard as a new email came in. Ryan. As if she needed another reminder of lost opportunities. Why hadn't she just taken him at his word and enjoyed the time they'd spent together instead of trying to pin him down to a commitment he couldn't or wouldn't give? The thumping of her heart felt loud enough to drown out the rain battering the kitchen window as she opened the message, but Wilma shuffling around trying to make herself comfortable appeared not to have heard.

Hi Chloe, apologies for not getting these to you sooner, but one way and another, I've been out of the picture. Quelle surprise, thought Chloe, a little cheered up by the possibility that Ryan hadn't been deliberately blanking her. *Ten photos as promised. Let me know if you need higher resolution images. I got your messages, thank you, although were you ringing with your head in a bucket? I couldn't make out exactly what you were saying only that Guy is a shit, but I thought you knew that. Also, I'm not sure how this is my fault. There's always my holiday cottage if you need a bolthole; I'm busy with a new project so you won't have to worry about bumping into me. Keys available, as previously, from my cousin, Tansy Connell, contact details below.*

Cheers,

Rx

PS Fred says hello to Wilma

Well, that was that. No hidden meaning. Short, to the point and a couple of polite noises, but mainly the sound of someone putting as much distance between them as possible. What had she expected? That Ryan would scoop her up and tell her he was changing his whole way of life on the strength of a stream of drunken gibberish? Really she had better things to do than rub salt into the wounds by downloading a series of images that would only remind her of everything she'd lost so that could wait. However, with the prospect of an estate agent appearing at any moment, there was one offer she was definitely going to take.

'Come on Wilma,' she said, holding her tight as she got to her feet. 'We're going on our holidays.'

13

It was with a huge sense of relief that Chloe loaded the car the next morning. In a way, it was a comfort to be heading back to where she would be surrounded by reminders of Ryan and of happier times in Little Spitmarsh. She tried not to torture herself wondering if his absence was by accident or design.

Before leaving, she cleaned her dad's house from top to bottom so that it was sparkling once again for the estate agent to show people round. Then, after weighing up when exactly the best time was to tell her dad and Emma that her plans for the future had gone so terribly wrong, sent her dad a brief summary of what happened and where she was. Finally, with Wilma safe and secure in her doggy car seat, she set off.

Chloe always enjoyed driving. She'd passed her test as soon as she could because her dad, whose mind was never on the task at hand, was such a terrible driver and she relished the independence that having her own car represented. The rain followed her all along the three hour journey to Little Spitmarsh, but it didn't matter because for once in her life the only thing she knew for certain was that the future was hers to decide. The squat, black-stained clapboard bungalow was just as she remembered it. Wilma seemed to know where she was too, giving a howl of anguish as they drove past Ryan's silent, shuttered Victorian house which brought a lump to Chloe's throat too.

'Fred's not here either,' Chloe told her, encouraging her gently through the front door. 'It's just you and me.' Someone had been in though, Ryan's cousin Tansy had popped over in advance of her arrival to turn on the heating and hot water and the wood burner glowed in friendly welcome. Chloe made a mental note to take her some flowers or a bottle of wine to say thank you. The other woman had been remarkably relaxed about Chloe's urgent request to rent the holiday bungalow and totally unruffled by her indecision about exactly how long she expected to stay.

'It doesn't matter,' Tansy assured her, with an amused toss of her bright curls as she'd handed the keys over. 'We'll talk about it when you've had a couple of days to unwind. It's not a problem, no one even thinks of coming here until the weather warms up. I'm afraid Little Spitmarsh isn't exactly Burnham Market or Holt, but I love it all the more for being relatively undiscovered. Of course it does have its own particular charms. My cousin Ryan's away at the moment, he'll be sorry not to have been able to greet you himself.'

Chloe gave her a sharp glance to see if she was making a deliberate link between the charms of Little Spitmarsh and Ryan, but the other woman's face was utterly without guile, although there was a mischievous twinkle in her eyes that suggested that she would make good company in different circumstances.

Wilma had recovered from her disappointment enough to stretch out in front of the stove so Chloe decided she could afford to sit down and relax with a mug of hot chocolate before taking her out for a walk. There was no pressure to do anything, no one else to worry about, yet she still felt compelled to reach for her laptop where Ryan's photos were tugging at her curiosity. The internet, she remembered, could be a bit sluggish here, this time, however, it connected immediately, but before she could open Ryan's message, her phone rang.

*   *   *

Ryan's heart sank as he drove slowly along the wide suburban street checking the numbers of the comfortable detached houses. He hoped he was mistaken, but as he drew up outside the address where Chloe lived with her dad, there was no doubting the 'for sale' board in the front garden. The house itself bore a distinctly closed look but flatly dismissing the possibility that he was too late, he hopped out of his seat and opened the back to release Fred from his harness. If Chloe didn't want to see him, she might at least grant visiting rights to Fred so that he could catch up with Wilma.

They had no sooner set foot on the drive when he heard the sound of another car door opening and closing, followed by the click of high heels moving swiftly towards them. 'Mr Barker?'

'Does she mean you, mate?' Ryan asked Fred.

He watched as a serious young woman in a blue business suit with her blonde hair swept off her face by an Alice band moved smartly ahead of them and planted herself, protectively, in the way of the front door. 'Deborah Dowling from Browns,' she said, offering her hand. 'Would you mind awfully leaving the dog in the car?'

'I'm sorry?'

She frowned. 'You are my twelve o'clock viewing aren't you?'

Ryan shook his head. 'I think one of us isn't supposed to be here.' He glanced at his phone to check again even though he was certain he'd found the right address. For a split-second he thought about pretending to be Mr Barker so he could gain entry and reassure himself that Chloe wasn't hiding inside, but his plan was rather spoilt by the arrival of an annoyed middle-aged man and a short, red-faced woman.

'I say,' the man said, crossly. 'I thought we had an exclusive viewing.'

'We're Mr and Mrs Barker,' the woman added, with a sense of entitlement. 'We understood we'd be first through the door once the owners had gone. We didn't think we'd signed up to an open day. How many more people have you lined up to see this house?'

Any last lingering glimmer of hope that he had found Chloe died. 'Don't mind me,' Ryan told the indignant Barkers. 'It's all yours. You're welcome to it.'

He trudged back to the jeep where a visibly perplexed Fred gave a moan of distress as he was clipped back into his harness. Ryan felt like joining in. He closed his eyes and thought about the conversation he'd had the day before when he'd been taking photos in the care home.

He'd been worried about disturbing Eva, who was eighty-eight, and had lung cancer, but she had been a very willing subject and keen to chat. 'I'm not dying,' she'd told him, with a smile that lit her still-lovely face, 'I'm living. I don't know if I'm counting my life in weeks or months, rightly enough, but I don't mind, you see, because it's all been so wonderful.'

Her eyes sparkled with pleasure when she talked about her family, and the years dropped from her face when she remembered her husband. 'I was married for fifty-nine sublimely happy years to the love of my life. People said we were polar opposites, that it would *never* last, but Peter and I proved them all wrong! Thank goodness we didn't have internet dating,' she said, laughing at the thought. 'Peter and I would never have been matched up, we both had *completely* different expectations of what we wanted from life, but I would have been so desperately miserable without him.'

Talking had made her very tired. Ryan dropped a light kiss on her cheek and whispered his thanks to her for making him realise how much time he had wasted. He'd gone home, packed a bag and gone off in search of Chloe. But where the hell was she? He rested his head on his arms on the steering wheel. 'Please Chloe,' he said out loud as he straightened up. 'Give me a sign. Tell me where you are, tell me that it's not too late.'

Then his phone rang.

'Tans?'

* ★ ★

The line crackled then cleared as Chloe heard a familiar voice. 'Dad? Where are you now? Are you okay?'

'Darling girl, I'm fine. We've reached Barbados. We're going snorkelling later and we're hoping to see turtles.'

'My goodness, Dad,' Chloe managed to splutter, having nearly choked on her hot chocolate. 'I'm amazed. You used to hate the sea! You'd never even come paddling with me. It was always Mum who had to brave the water when we went to the seaside.'

There was a pause which suggested the weak connection had been lost, but then she heard him clear his throat. 'Forgive me, my darling,' he croaked, 'I really haven't been much of a father to you. I've been so selfish. I let your poor mother do all the parenting, all the broken nights, all the nappies, all the colds and sickness bugs. I'm afraid I was an absolute coward about all the aspects of dealing with a baby. My work

211

provided an easy excuse for not having to get my hands dirty.'

'Dad,' she murmured, 'it's all in the past. None of that matters now.'

'It does because I still blame myself for what happened to your mother. If I'd supported her then, she might not have . . . '

'Mum was ill,' she insisted quietly. 'It wasn't your fault that she took her own life.'

'Maybe not, Chloe, but I've betrayed her memory by failing to take care of you. I should have been more hands-on, shown you how much I love you. *Told* you how very precious you are to me . . . then perhaps you wouldn't have rushed into the arms of that oleaginous, pompous, self-obsessed creep, Guy Bradshaw.'

Despite herself, Chloe chuckled. 'Not a fan then, Dad?'

'I didn't like him from the start, but I thought you could see something about him that I just wasn't getting. Emma and I couldn't be happier that you've given him the push. You just seemed so *resigned* to being with him, as if it was your duty to be his partner, rather than your desire. Real love isn't about trying to put up with someone, it's about discovering a life full of promise. Together.'

'I'm so pleased that's what you've found, Dad,' she said, wishing she could give him a hug. 'It's lovely of you to check up on me, but I'm fine, so go and find Emma and enjoy the rest of your honeymoon.'

'Not so fast, young lady,' he put in quickly, 'Emma and I have been talking and there's something we'd like to do.'

Her hot chocolate had gone cold by the time she'd absorbed what her father had to say. Chloe exhaled slowly. She'd always found reasons to excuse his rather detached manner and resisted any temptation to label him as selfish, but here he was admitting as much and trying to put things right in a way she could never have anticipated.

'Oh Dad,' she told him, firmly, 'I did

it for love, there's no charge.' Nevertheless there would be lots to talk about when he and Emma returned from their honeymoon, with more honesty on both sides and a fresh start all round.

Her chocolate refreshed, Chloe armed herself with her turquoise silk covered notebook which she'd bought in Hong Kong. So far she hadn't quite found the courage to re-read her diary of the trip because her impressions of the city were so bound up with her feelings for Ryan that it would be painful to relive them. Still, she would need her notes to do justice to Ryan's images, especially if he was pitching the combination to magazines. However blasé Ryan seemed to be about money, as a freelance photographer his reputation rested on everything associated with his name.

Chloe prepared herself as the broadband ground slowly into action. Her breath caught as the pixelated images struggled to resolve themselves only to blur again as tears welled up and slid slowly down her cheeks. From the beginning, she'd admired Ryan's work for its narrative quality, but he also had a way of revealing the smallest details and capturing the magic of the moment; a bleak moorland bathed in a pool of gold at the foot of rainbow, silver mist rising from a sapphire-blue waterfall, a crescent moon hanging above snow-covered mountain peaks in an amber dawn.

But this was written especially for her; their story in ten images. There she was in black and white, dark hair fanning out from her face as she turned to the camera laughing as she held up a melting ice cream. Little Spitmarsh's old-fashioned sea front had been searingly hot that day, and they'd splashed in the waves like carefree teenagers.

The next frame caught her with the bed sheets pulled up to her chin, her face flushed with love. Ryan had gone out to make breakfast and she'd only just managed to pull the covers up in time to hide her modesty when he sneaked back to take a picture of her.

Here were Fred and Wilma curled up together in Fred's basket and then a sad shot of Fred staring at an empty space. Chloe scrolled through, her tears unchecked, as she saw herself set against the backdrop of Hong Kong; a shot of her in sunglasses, spreading her arms as she took in the panoramic views from Victoria Peak, another of her smiling happily on the Star Ferry, then looking pensive at the Good Wish Gardens. All captured at moments when she was unaware of the camera but all bearing the same message, that Ryan thought she was beautiful, that she was someone he cared for deeply. Finally, in case she hadn't understood his meaning, the last shot, a heart scrawled in the sand just as the tide was coming up to wash the message away. 'I miss you.'

How unfair of her to think he used the camera as a barrier between the world and his feelings when his photographs couldn't be more revealing. A thousand words, that's what he'd asked for in return. She was pretty sure she only needed three.

14

Chloe needed to burn off her nervous excitement so she hurried out for an early walk to the creek the next morning. The mild wet weather had given way to a cold front overnight so that the peachy dawn caught the diamond dusting of ice on the wooden pontoon as she picked her way to the end with Wilma shivering and protesting at her side.

'Don't be such a wimp, the fresh air's good for you. Besides, you need to get used to bracing weather as you'll be getting far more of it.'

Having decided she'd put too much of her life on hold guarding herself against an uncertain future, Chloe intended to make the most of every moment from now on. She hugged herself, watching a pale path of light widen on the amethyst waters of Campion's Creek. She checked her watch and wondered if it was too soon to return to the cottage, when every fibre of her body suddenly became alert to the sound of approaching footsteps.

A slight vibration in the planks beneath her feet made her turn and the cold air and the sudden thumping of her heart made her breath erratic. The tall, brawny man coming towards her was missing a lot of hair and beard, but, as he drew nearer he was even more handsome than she remembered. She was getting to her feet when a large basset came thundering towards her and nearly knocked her over in his haste to get to Wilma.

'Here you are at last.' Ryan's voice was husky with emotion, 'I was worried when I couldn't find you at the cottage.'

'I didn't think you'd be back this early,' she said, keeping a check on her urge to fling herself at him.

'I've been everywhere looking for you.' He studied her face intently. 'When I sent the photos to you and you didn't reply, I almost gave up hope. Then, when I was at work, I had a reminder about the things in life that matter most.'

Perhaps even Ryan could have too much of his own company, she dared to think.

'I'd already lost you twice because I'd been too dumb to tell you how I felt about you. I didn't want to lose you forever so I went to look for you. I tried your work and found out you'd left, I went to your Dad's home and saw a 'for sale' board outside. The last place I thought to look was where I started; I didn't really think that you would use the holiday cottage. So when Tansy rang and told me you'd turned up here, all I wanted to do was get back before you took fright again.'

'But I messaged you!'

'Yes,' he smiled. 'That's when I started to think there might be a chance for me. I would have driven back yesterday, but the double journey would have been too tiring for Fred, although I can't say I got much rest.'

She was about to reach out to him but he drew back for a moment, indicating that she should hear him out. Chloe waited in agony while he struggled to compose himself. Fatigue had drained his face of colour except for his dark eyes which were red-rimmed with sleeplessness.

'I've been thinking about what's really important to me,' he continued just as she was on the point of putting her hands up to his face and telling him that he didn't owe her any explanation. 'I've been taking photographs recently in one of the local old folks' homes. It began as a birthday surprise for one of the residents but what I didn't anticipate was that *I* would learn so much from the experience.'

'In what way?' she asked quietly.

He smiled. 'Well, for a start, it's crystallised some thoughts I've been having about the importance of home and not wanting to go away so much. But also because the old people I've chatted to have such a wealth of knowledge and their own unique histories — yet all of them are in danger of being forgotten. As you'd expect, not many of them are leaving digital footprints behind them! So it gave me the idea of doing something to capture the essence of those personalities, to celebrate their collected wisdom before it's too late. There's a charity that helps old people to connect, especially those who are socially isolated and I'm going to do some work with them. Seeing people confined to their beds, listening to their stories and knowing that many of them have no one but strangers to care for them was a powerful reminder of what's really precious. I can't promise I'm never going to climb another mountain, but if I stay closer to home Chloe, will you give me another chance?'

Chloe looked at him and felt her stomach lurch. 'No. Sorry Ryan, that's no basis for a relationship because,' she added quickly, seeing him flinch, 'I can't keep you against your will or on a leash. You don't need to make any promises to me; it's not the future that's important, it's now, it's this moment we should cherish. I'll never stop you doing what you need to do.'

'What I need to do,' he said, stepping forwards and putting his arms around her. 'Is to be with you, to explore the future together. But what about you?'

'You saw the estate agent's board outside my parents' house? Well, my dad's promised me a share of the proceeds of the sale. He's says it's what my mother would have wanted for me and to make up, apparently, for being too wrapped up in his own grief to notice mine. So I can put a deposit on a house, or resume my studies, or do whatever I want within reason. Suddenly anything's possible.'

Ryan searched her face, his dark eyes serious. 'I'm glad. That'll give you a sense of security.'

Chloe shook her head and laughed. 'Not really. Not when it comes to saying something important to someone who's shown me how to treasure the small moments in life not just the big things. I'm still afraid of looking silly, being rejected or feeling a failure.'

'Ah, go on, you just need a bit of encouragement,' Ryan said softly.

Chloe felt the warmth spreading through her as he bent his head towards her and pressed his lips to hers, sweet and soft at first and then more hungrily as she ran her hands over his face and through his hair. They kissed in a moment of pure happiness that felt as if it would stretch into infinity, except that Chloe still had Wilma's lead attached to her wrist and Wilma, flirting shamelessly with Fred was running rings around them threatening to pull them both over.

'It might be easier,' she said, laughing as she and Ryan tried to untie themselves, 'if I just let go of this end while we . . . '

As Chloe skipped over an excited Wilma, the lead dropped out of her hand. Wilma, sensing freedom, made a wild leap for Fred then there was a splash and she disappeared into Campion's Creek.

Chloe heard herself scream and then

there was another crash of water as Ryan shrugged off his jacket and jumped off the pontoon. Was she about to lose both of them? Chloe squeezed her eyes shut until she heard Ryan telling her it was safe to look.

'It's a big spring tide,' he pointed out, standing up in water that came up to his thighs, Wilma drenched but unharmed in his arms. 'We were never going to have to swim for it.' Passing Wilma carefully to Chloe, he hopped back onto the pontoon and picked up his jacket to wrap round the shivering dachshund whilst a frantic Fred ran up and down beside them.

'Now do I need to tell you how much I love you?' he asked, pointing to his wet clothes.

'No,' said Chloe, 'because you were written in my stars. It's what the fortune teller told me, that I'd know you by the four-legged creature and the dark water.'

She looked down at Wilma, gazing adoringly at Fred and the waters of

Campion's Creek glimmering gunmetal-grey in the morning light. Then she gazed straight into Ryan's face and there was no mistaking all the love in his unguarded emotions without the protection of a camera lens. He smiled and held out his hand and her skin tingled with the magic of the moment as their fingertips touched. Two children, the fortune teller had told her, but she was glad she didn't know what exactly came next because she was looking forward to finding out. Tomorrow was for adventures and catching moonbeams in a jar, but for now they had something far more tangible to explore. She slipped her hand in Ryan's and together they herded the two dogs back along the pontoon towards the foreshore, to home and to happiness.

Thank you

Hello! Given all the demands on everyone's time, I won't keep you but I do want to say a huge thank you for reading *Moonbeams In A Jar*. I'm a very visual writer in the sense that ideas often come to me like still pictures from a film and this a story I've wanted to write since I 'saw' Chloe sitting at the end of a wooden pontoon with Wilma, her dachshund, beside her. How, I wondered, could I make her and the handsome bearded man heading towards her with his dog, Fred, see that they were right for each other? I also love writing about places; I've been lucky enough to visit Hong Kong, I've been soaked to the skin climbing in Snowdonia and, of course, Little Spitmarsh, the sleepy seaside town inspired by my sailing experiences is somewhere very dear to me. I hope this book has given you a flavour of those locations and that you've enjoyed accompanying Chloe and Ryan on their travels.

All journeys — and novels — come to an end, but before you think about your next destination, please could I ask a small favour? Reviews really do make a difference — I can't tell you how much a kind review brightens my day and raises the profile of the book. So, please, if you have a moment, I'd really appreciate it if you could leave a brief review on the site where you bought this book or somewhere like Goodreads. Thank you so much for your time.

With warm wishes,
Chris x

We do hope that you have enjoyed reading this large print book.

Did you know that all of our titles are available for purchase?

We publish a wide range of high quality large print books including:
Romances, Mysteries, Classics
General Fiction
Non Fiction and Westerns

Special interest titles available in large print are:
The Little Oxford Dictionary
Music Book, Song Book
Hymn Book, Service Book

Also available from us courtesy of Oxford University Press:
Young Readers' Dictionary
(large print edition)
Young Readers' Thesaurus
(large print edition)

For further information or a free brochure, please contact us at:
Ulverscroft Large Print Books Ltd.,
The Green, Bradgate Road, Anstey,
Leicester, LE7 7FU, England.
Tel: (00 44) **0116 236 4325**
Fax: (00 44) **0116 234 0205**

Other titles in the
Linford Romance Library:

ROMANTIC DOCTOR

Phyllis Mallett

1968: As a doctor at St Jermyn's Hospital, Ann Barling's work is her life, and it seems like romance has passed her by completely. She may as well admit to herself that she's now a confirmed spinster. When she returns to work after a holiday, however, change is afoot in the form of newly hired Dr David Hanbury. He has a reputation, and seems determined to add Ann to his list of conquests. But she's having none of it . . .